NORTHERN FLAMES

A Novel

'The brightest flame casts the darkest shadow.'
Game of Thrones

Quirinal Press

Copyright © Ian Thomson 2021

Ian Thomson has asserted his right under the Copyright,
Designs and Patents Act 1988 to be identified as the author of this work

This book is a work of fiction. The characters within it are not intended
to represent any persons, living or dead. Any apparent resemblance
is purely coincidental.

Cover image (copyright pending) with thanks to
Blackburn Fire Service
and the kind permission of the
Editor of the *Lancashire Telegraph*

DEDICATED TO

Queen Elizabeth's Grammar School
Blackburn

IMPORTANT NOTE
Do not skip

This really is a work of fiction. None of the characters exists or has ever existed outside the pages of this novel. None of the events described at St John's church or school or at QEGS ever happened. Descriptions of Blackburn are faithful or at least as I remember the town as I was growing up. One or two minor liberties may have been taken for the sake of the fiction. Equally, though I have drawn on memories to construct the story, it is not an autobiography. Now read on.

1. BLACKPOOL

'COME ON, STEWPOT!' Ben whispered. 'He's not looking.'

Ben was on the other side of the red silk rope looped onto brass rings at the top of the stairs.

I looked over my shoulder at the commissionaire in his plum-coloured uniform, decorated with grubby gold braid. He was standing at the entrance to the waxworks, having a crafty fag, and staring out at the grey, bad-tempered sea. He had his back to us and seemed completely absorbed.

'Come on, yer daft ha'porth!' Ben hissed. 'Stop dithering.'

I took my chance and slipped under the rope and we tiptoed down the steps to the

Anatomical Museum
Adults only

When you're a pair of twelve-year-old lads, and somebody puts up a sign saying 'Adults Only' - well, it's like issuing an invitation, isn't it? If somebody puts up a sign saying 'Keep Out!' - you go in, don't you? You have to. It's nature.

There was me, Stuart 'Stewpot' Cooper and my best mate, Ben 'Bendytoy' Westwell. We called him that after a popular kind of soft toy at the time. There was Mickey Mouse, Donald Duck, Popeye, all sorts. You could bend their limbs into weird positions and they would stay that way because of stiff wire inside.

We used to do this to Ben in St John's graveyard before Evensong. We would bend his arm so his elbow was sticking out and lift one leg so his knee was in the air and then we'd twist his head round as far as it would go. Whatever strange position you put him in, he'd stay there. He was a good sort was Ben.

They called me 'Stewpot' because all Stuarts get called Stewpot.

Anyway, here we were on the choir trip to Blackpool. The previous year, we'd been to York for our annual treat, which was all right, because you could walk all the way round the city on the medieval walls. But once you'd done that, to be honest, it was a bit boring. We had a look at the Minster, of course, and I have to admit it was pretty impressive, bigger than St John's any road. What I liked best was the massive golden dragon just sticking out of the wall really high up. I mean it was just weird, like it had been coming through the wall and it got stuck. It was looking upwards as if it was wriggling to get in through the wall and then the archbishop cursed it and it got frozen so it couldn't get into the cathedral. It was stuck halfway in - for ever.

Mr Butterfield, our choirmaster and the organist at St John's, had a leaflet and he said the dragon was probably part of the lifting mechanism for the lid of a font which wasn't there any more. I could see that it might be like a fancy version of the jib cranes that stuck out of factory walls along the Blakewater and along the canal back in Blackburn, but I preferred my version of the story.

Anyway, we had a cathedral of our own in Blackburn. Me and Ben had sung there once at a festival for East Lancashire choirs. It was not as big, not by a long way, but it was ours. The one with the dragon had the disadvantage of being in Yorkshire, the wrong side of the Pennines as far as we were concerned.

Anyway, this wasn't our idea of the perfect day out. We had choir practice on Thursday and at least two services on Sundays so going to see another kind of church, no matter how big or beautiful, wasn't much of a thrill.

Mr Butterfield was a good man and a kind man, and perhaps he'd sensed our mild disappointment because the following year he actually asked us where we'd like to go.

'Blackpool!' we shouted.

If I remember rightly, we were pretty well unanimous. It was Mr Butterfield's turn to look mildly disappointed, but he was a man of his word and he made the arrangements.

The sun was shining in Blackburn on the morning of the trip. The statue of Queen Victoria on the Boulevard gleamed (and, for once, she didn't have a waste bin on her head); the green double-decker buses gleamed; I dare say our well-scrubbed faces gleamed as well. Sunbeams even leaked through holes in the roof of the soot-blackened station with its massive Victorian clocks and the model of the Isle of Man steamer in a glass case. There was a blaze of sunshine at either end of our gloomy platform where pigeons were moaning and squabbling on the iron girders above us.

They scattered in panic at a shrill whistle from the engine which came hissing and chuffing into the station. Smoke and steam went billowing into the vault above and rolled back down. There was a squeal of brakes as the engine came to a halt and then a long, soft sigh as more steam came out from above the wheels and went rolling across the platform around our ankles. Mr Butterfield said the train had come across the Pennines from York. We were secretly glad it would be continuing in the opposite direction.

There was no corridor in the carriages and there was a scramble to get into a carriage that Mr Butterfield and his wife were *not* getting into. As we moved off there was a cheer from all the lads. Me and Ben managed to get a compartment to ourselves and Ben used the leather strap to lower the window. We passed through Mill Hill and Cherry Tree out into the open countryside and the deep wooded gorge by Hoghton Tower. We waved to people at level crossings and on bridges and we even waved to cows and sheep.

The weather began to change once we were beyond Preston. Thick grey clouds began to mass and blot out the sun. As we hung out of the window, we could see that where the coast must be, the grey clouds were turning a dense black and, sure enough, before long, cold raindrops began to hit our faces. We had to sit down, close the window and abandon our game of 'First-to-spot-Blackpool-Tower'. The raindrops chasing each other down the window, as we crossed the flatlands of the Fylde, dampened our spirits a little but we were determined to enjoy ourselves, and enjoy ourselves we would. Besides, Mr Butterfield had checked the weather forecast and told us this might happen, but that it was set to brighten up in the afternoon.

By the time we reached Blackpool North Station, it was raining heavily and there was a brisk wind. Some of the boys had brought their school macs, some were happy to get wet but me and Ben had Pac-a-macs, thin lightweight plastic raincoats that could be folded into a small parcel. Mine was transparent green and Bendytoy's was girly pink.

'It's me mum's,' he said. It came down to his ankles and he had to roll the sleeves up.

'You look like a big girl's blouse,' I said.

2.　　THE GOLDEN MILE

WE TROOPED DOWN TO THE SEA FRONT near the North Pier. The rain had eased a bit but the wind was fierce and came at us in buffets which threatened to knock us off our feet.

But we could see the Tower now and ran towards it, crouching in the wind. When Mr and Mrs Butterfield had caught up with us and we were standing under the canopy outside the building, he said:

'Right, in a minute you can go off on your own but listen to me carefully or we go straight back home. Do you hear me?'

'Yes, Mr Butterfield,' we chanted in unison.

'Now, I want you back here at twelve noon on the dot,' he said. 'I'll have some dinner money for you. Have you got that?'

'Yes, Mr Butterfield!' we sang out again.

'When I've checked that you're all present and correct, you're free again until three o'clock. Sam and Tim will stay with me and Mrs Butterfield. Nigel Clitheroe, are you listening to me, boy?'

Sam and Tim were probationers in the choir. They didn't wear surplices yet and were learning on the job. They were only eight, bless 'em. Nigel Clitheroe was a right cloth-head. As Mr B was giving his instructions, Nigel was looking up at the tower with his head so far back, he looked as if it would fall off the back of his neck and roll over the tramlines.

'What?' he said. 'Er, no...yes...what?'

'Good gracious,' Mr Butterfield said. 'Somebody sort him, will you? I want you back here at three o'clock sharp. I've got tickets for the Zoo and then the Circus, and if you're late we won't get in.

'Now pay attention. Do not go anywhere near the sea wall in this wind. The tide's in and it's dangerous. A boy and his dog were swept away a couple of years ago, and were not seen again until they were washed up dead in Lytham days later. Have you got that? Everybody? Nigel?'

'Sir!' Nigel squawked after a sharp dig in the ribs from Ben.

'Now, Mrs Butterfield and I are going in search of a nice cup of tea. Off you go and behave!'

The last two words were whipped away by the wind as we scattered in all directions like startled sheep. Some raced ahead to the Golden Mile, some disappeared into sweet shops, and some went back to check out the North Pier. I had been to Blackpool several times with my mum and dad and I knew my way around. I knew that the North Pier was a bit boring and led Ben down towards Central Pier which was much more lively.

On the way we stopped off at a souvenir shop to buy rock. Ben bought a key-ring with his name on it. They didn't have one with a 'Stuart' tag, but I was itching to buy something, so I bought a thimble with a picture of Blackpool Tower on it for my mum.

We spent a while, as we waited for the weather to change, snorting and giggling at the range of saucy picture postcards on a revolving rack. They were all about bums and tits and terrible puns. I remember a fat man in a striped bathing suit whose belly was so big it cast a shadow. In the shadow a small boy was licking an ice cream. The man was shading his eyes with one hand and saying: 'I wish I could see my little Willy'.

There were scenes in doctors' surgeries with jokes about 'just a little prick' or 'having a bun in the oven'. There were sex-starved little men marooned on desert islands. There were scenes on the promenade and on the beach and in the sea, featuring little red-nosed, hen-pecked husbands and their enormous wives with bosoms like balloons. There were glamour girls with tiny skirts lifted by the wind to reveal blushing bottoms. There were Scotsmen in kilts which were also lifted by the sea breeze to reveal hairy backsides. There were drunks with noses on fire, policemen and vicars. I remember one card in particular: two elderly women with pinched faces are passing an open window.

'There's the vicar at the window sponging his aspidistra,' says one.

'Horrid man,' says the other. 'He ought to do it in the bathroom out of sight.'

This was so daft that we clutched each other helplessly and nearly wet ourselves with laughing.

'Oy, you two!' shouted the fat lady behind the counter. She could have stepped out of one of the postcards. 'Bugger off if you're not buying! You've had your sticky hands all over them cards. Now, go on, clear off out of it!'

We scampered off. The rain was thinning and the sky was lightening to the south. A line of bright blue was becoming wider under the dark clouds. This was the direction in which we were heading, with the Pleasure Beach our ultimate destination.

We took a detour into an amusement arcade and played a shove penny game for a while with no luck whatsoever. We weren't tempted to stay long because we knew these places were for suckers and we weren't going to throw our brass away. We'd saved for this: Ben had a paper round and I had a generous grandma. In addition there were our choir tips.

We had sung at a funeral recently. We preferred funerals to weddings. Ben said weddings were a bit childish. They always started with the Wedding March and then there'd be: *Dear Lord and Father of mankind/Forgive our foolish ways,* which Ben said was asking for trouble. Either that or *Amazing Grace,* which Ben said was like 'dying bagpipes'. An admittedly weird couple once asked for *Give me Oil in my Lamp,* for which Ben had a rude interpretation. He once got a right bollocking for laughing at the bit in the service where the vicar says that marriage was instituted by God for the avoidance of fornication. Apparently the bride had been very upset, which nearly set Ben off again.

'Man that is born of a woman hath but a short time to live,' was more our style. 'He cometh up, and is cut down, like a flower.' That stuff. It was grim but only like *The Twilight Zone* on the telly. Of course, the coffin would be lying in the chancel and Ben would make ghoulish faces at me from the choir stalls at the other side, but there was no real fear. We were children after all and we thought ourselves immortal.

In any case, the music was more interesting. *Abide with me* is a fantastic hymn and *The Lord is my Shepherd* is a lovely psalm. Sometimes there'd be an anthem which we'd have to learn in advance.

If I'm honest, the real reason we preferred funerals to weddings was that the going rate for weddings was a shilling, whereas for funerals it was two and six.

So, if we were wary of blowing our lolly, we weren't totally against the idea of a bit of gambling, and were drawn to the Bingo stall near the front of the arcade. We sat on high stools at screens with numbers on. You were supposed to slide a plastic tab over your number if it was called. We knew the calls:

> *On its own: number 1*
> *Key of the door: 21*
> *Legs 11: Number 11*
> *Two fat ladies: 88*
> *Lucky for some: number 13*
> - and so on.

But nothing was happening. The caller sat on his high stool with his head buried in *The Sun*.

'Hey, Mister,' Ben said. 'When are you going to start?'

The man looked up, stared at us, picked something from his teeth and returned to his paper.

We sat there for about ten minutes.

Eventually an old lady with a bald patch, a crocheted cardigan, and a few items of shopping in a string bag, came up to us.

'Tha's wastin' thi time, cockles,' she said to us. 'He won't start a game till he has a full deck of punters. And he's a mardy old sod, any road.'

'And you can get stuffed an' all, you daft bat,' the man said without looking up.

The woman gave him a V sign and went off cackling.

We slid off our stools.

The sun was coming out.

A little further down the front we found Louis Tussaud's Waxworks.

The Chamber of Horrors lured us in.

3. THE WAXWORKS

ACTUALLY, THE CHAMBER OF HORRORS was a big disappointment. It's true there was no shortage of medieval instruments of torture. There was a wax man being stretched on the rack, and though his face was twisted in agony the fact that the features were motionless wasn't the least bit convincing. There was a guillotine and a headless victim stretched out on it, near a basket of severed heads, but the neck was not spouting blood. It just looked like a bit of scrag end from the butcher's. There was a lot more of this pathetic stuff in various tableaux, dimly lit in a red glow. Shrieks and screams and wails of agony came through a sound system, and we found them hilarious until Ben started howling himself. He was much scarier than the museum's sound track.

The Gallery of Fame was even worse. Some of the figures were a better likeness than others but I thought the deadness of the eyes was even creepier than the Chamber of Horrors. There was the Queen, of course, and Prince Philip, and Harold Macmillan and

Harold Wilson. There were Petula Clark and Alma Cogan and Shirley Bassey with rigid smiles and tight sequinned dresses.

I put Ben in full Bendytoy mode and he took on the attitude of Mr Churchill with his cigar. Then I made him strike the hip-swivel pose of Elvis the Pelvis.

But we soon got bored.

That's why our illegal foray down into the Anatomy Museum was so exciting. We waited at the bottom of the stairs for a few minutes to see if anyone had noticed us trespassing, but it was OK. The place was totally empty owing to the rain earlier. At the bottom of the stairs was a billboard announcing the treasures within:

ANATOMY
EXHIBITS
from the
LIVERPOOL MUSEUM
&

THE NEW SCHOOL OF HYGIENE
from
DRESDEN

Includes FREE

Admission to:
THE SENSATIONAL
VISIBLE
Electronic
GLASS WOMAN
and
GLASS MAN
From
behind the
Iron Curtain

THIS SUPERB COLLECTION
comprising
upwards of 1,000 Models and Diagrams
Was
Procured at the
Anatomical Galleries of Paris, Florence and Munich.

Wide-eyed, we passed the billboard into Room 1. Standing on either side of us were the glass man and woman. I think they must have been made of various kinds of plastic rather than glass but I have to admit they were pretty impressive. Through the glass you could see the white bones and dark pink twisted cords of muscles and the red arteries and blue veins. It was like the pull-out diagrams in my St John Ambulance guide book, but in three dimensions.

Beyond these figures were various windows built into the walls, behind which were sections of the human body, made out of wax presumably, which showed various organs such as the heart, kidneys and liver. They were clever, but a bit boring unless you wanted to be a doctor. We didn't. Ben wanted to be a fireman and I wanted to be an astronaut. Ben achieved his ambition in a way, I suppose, but my future career was more down to earth.

There were also a number of glass cases. Case No. 2 was deeply weird and fascinating. It seemed to have nothing whatsoever to do with anything else in the museum and its contents seemed to have nothing whatsoever to do with each other. The case contained:

72. Skeleton of a Viper
73. Model of a Colorado Beetle
74. Model of a tongue, actual size, having syphilitic ulcers at root of tonsils
75. Head of a Mummy, brought from the Royal Catacombs
76. Ends of the Fingers of a Hand laid open showing the nerves

77. Calculus stone found in the Bladder of a man
78. A specimen of the King Crab
79. Skeleton and Skull of a Tortoise
80. Original skull of a prehistoric animal
81. A White Wasps' nest
82. Skeleton of an English Bat
83. Genuine Alligator
84. The Head of a New Zealand chief. The skin of his face has been elaborately tattooed

This was fascinating stuff which prompted Ben to go through his full repertoire of faces. You couldn't be anywhere near Ben in the classroom when he started pulling these faces. Once, in Maths, I saw him stick his jaw out so his bottom teeth were showing, he crossed his eyes, and stuck his earlobes in his ears. I gave an involuntary snort of laughter, which earned me a detention while he got away scot-free.

We giggled like maniacs at these items although we had to suppress our hysteria because we weren't supposed to be there. The effort had snot blowing out of one of Ben's nostrils and I froze while he blew his nose and wiped it clean as quietly as he could.

'Whose royal catacombs?' he gasped. 'The Queen's?'

'What prehistoric animal?' I whispered.

'Looks like a post-historic sheep to me,' Ben said. 'There's one just like it in the art room at school. Hey, what's so special about an English bat?'

'Talks posh?' I said. 'Plays cricket?'

'Very funny,' Ben said. 'What's genuine about that alligator? Looks like a newt to me.'

'The tattooed guy is pretty fab, though,' I said.

'Well, yeah, maybe,' Ben said. 'If he's not just *papier mâché.*'

Case No. 4 contained a 'Dissected hen and eggs'. We were unimpressed.

Case No. 6 was something else.

This case was horizontal and contained the wax model of a kid of about our age with his innards cut away. The label read:

EXTRAORDINARY FREAK OF NATURE OF A MAN BEING DISCOVERED IN THE 'FAMILY WAY'

Clearly visible in the abdomen of the boy was a well-developed foetus.

'Jeepers creepers!' Ben said. 'He's preggers!'

We read the explanation greedily.

'When this unfortunate child was begotten,' it read, 'a twin was begotten at the same time; but while the brother formed in the usual way, the impregnated egg of his sister lay dormant; and without resistance became closed up within the brother's abdomen. These living rudiments lay quiet for a few years - so within the body of the brother the impregnated egg lay, and then formation commencing, the young man became pregnant with his twin sister and the wonder and catastrophe (death) ensued. N.B - This model is protected by Act of Parliament.'

'Fuck me!' I said.

'Nah,' Ben said. 'You might get a bun in the oven, like him.'

This led to a bout of suppressed hysteria so severe that we had to crouch on the floor behind the coffin-shaped exhibit because we thought we'd heard a noise on the stairs.

When we were sure that all was quiet again and we'd stopped gasping for breath, we moved on.

Case No. 7 contained a model of a young lady - showing the result of 'Tight Lacing'. The result appeared to be an 18 inch waist and crushed internal organs. Ben pulled one of his most eloquent faces.

Case No. 9 contained a Coelacanth, for no coherent reason.

We had arrived now at the doorway to Room 2. Above the lintel was a notice in ferocious red lettering:

Adult Only Section
Persons Under 16 <u>Not</u> Admitted

So, of course we went in.

There were models of the pelvic organs of a man and of a woman but we'd looked up all this sort of stuff in an encyclopaedia in the school Library. The same with the models of the menstrual cycle which brought on Ben's I'm-about-to-throw-up face. Actually, we prided ourselves that we knew all there was to know about, you know, S-E-X, though I'd had to correct Ben's conviction that a girl would get pregnant automatically *unless* she had sex at least once a month. I did this by making him read the relevant entry in the encyclopaedia properly. He seemed quite disappointed - perhaps he was dimly aware that the truth might spoil some future chat-up line.

There was a lot of this purely mechanical stuff which did nothing whatsoever to titillate us - quite the reverse if anything. There was a lot of frankly gruesome stuff about childbirth which we knew about. It was described as a 'miracle' but left me feeling queasy.

There was more interesting stuff ahead. There were models of the sexual parts of hermaphrodites which made Ben's jaw drop till he looked completely gormless. I found them horribly fascinating too.

Then my attention was taken up with a number of cases showing the effects of syphilis. Human faces '-from infancy to old age - showing secondary symptoms of syphilis and gonorrhoea in all their frightful forms.' There were horrible sores and eyes weeping pus and noses half-eaten away. It was much better than the Chamber of Horrors.

And there were cabinets with willies and front bottoms covered with horrible pimples and pustules.

Ben had gone ahead.

'Come here quick,' he hissed.

He had found a set of cabinets labelled: 'Masturbation'.

We looked at 'the face of an old bachelor; a confirmed onanist. He became idiotic and rapidly sank into second childhood,' said the notice.

Half of his face had sort of collapsed and one side of his mouth and one eye had slid downwards. In retrospect, I think he must have suffered a stroke but I didn't know about such things at the time.

'How did they know?' Ben asked.

'How did they know what?' I said.

'How did they know that he was a wanker?'

The giggles started rising again.

There were a few more cases in this section showing male genitals supposedly distorted by self-abuse. Some had become bloated and some had shrunk like the end of a deflated balloon - but the last exhibit was just too much. The penis was as thin and as elongated as a piece of string and came down to the poor victim's knees.

It was too much.

We burst into shrieks of crazy laughter which brought the commissionaire thundering down the stairs. He chased us around the exhibits but we were young and fit and he was old and fat, and we easily escaped and ran out onto the prom where the sun was shining brightly and drying up the puddles.

'Oh God, look at the time,' Ben said, consulting his watch. 'We'll be late for roll call and Buttercup will lose his rag.'

We broke into a trot.

'Stewpot,' Ben said, 'you behave yourself in bed tonight - or you'll get a spaghetti willy.'

4. BEN HAS HIS FORTUNE TOLD

BY THE TIME WE MET UP WITH THE OTHERS, we weren't late at all, even though we were the last to arrive. Mr Butterfield had a surprise for us all. Five bob each! Two shiny half crowns! He said the churchwardens had a special collection each year for the Choristers' Day Out. I didn't remember this happening at York or, if it did, it certainly wasn't such a princely sum. I'd always thought of thc churchwardens as a grumpy lot but I resolved to change my mind and be more polite from now on.

'Right,' Mr Butterfield said, obviously delighted at the reception of his little surprise, 'back here at three o'clock sharp or you'll spoil it for the others.'

Mrs B was beaming as if she'd just given birth to us all.

'Bang on three, mind! Off you go!'

But we were already zooming off down the sea front.

The tide was going out, revealing the famous golden sands. Once we were free of the others, we bought a six of chips each and sat on the sea wall to eat them. Though it was sunny now, the wind was still brisk and we laughed at men in their Sunday suits struggling with wind breaks and deckchairs. Dogs chased each other wildly along the waterline. Small children were busy on sandcastles soon to be decorated with paper flags: the Welsh dragon, the Scottish Saltire, the cross of St. George and the Irish harp. The donkeys were being brought out in a line. Ben, who'd been on a real horse in the Trough of Bowland, sniffed at the idea of a donkey ride and was amused to see that the doziest looking one had a label over his nose which said: 'Flash'.

'Look!' Ben said, pointing.

There was a cluster of boys from our choir at the water's edge. They were jostling and pushing each other. Then suddenly, Kenneth Buck - you could tell Kenneth's red hair a mile off - started taking his clothes off till he was down to his baggy underpants. He was daft as a brush was Kenneth. As he rushed into the sea we could see the others jumping up and down with glee.

He swam quite a way out, to be fair, before he turned back. He came walking out of the water with his shoulders hunched and his hands held out by his sides. Even at this distance, we could see him mouthing: 'IT'S COLD'.

Once back on the beach, he peeled off his wet underpants, whirled them around his head and threw
them at the others, who began throwing them backwards and forwards to one another. As Kenneth pulled
on his jeans, a Jack Russell intercepted his pants and
ran off with them, with the boys in hot pursuit and
Ken hopping after them.

'What a load of divs,' Ben said, laughing. 'Come on
you, if you've finished them chips.'

We crossed the tramlines and resumed our exped-
ition down the Golden Mile.

The air was full of the sickly smell of candy floss
and doughnuts, the sweet reek of fried onions from
hot dog stalls and the tang of frying fish. We stopped
at a stall to watch Blackpool Rock being pulled. Ben
asked the man how he got the letters in Blackpool
Rock and the man said:

'Do you know how many times a day I'm asked
that question?'

'I dunno,' said Ben. 'How many?'

'Dosta know how many fish are in that sea, cock?'

'No, I don't,' Ben said. 'Nobody does.'

'Well, it's that many times.'

'How do you do it, though?'

'How do I do what?'

'Get the bloomin' letters in Blackpool Rock?'

'Well, lad,' the man said with a broad grin. 'That's for me to know and thee to find out. Trade secret that is, son. Are you buying or what?'

'We had some not long since,' Ben said and we moved on.

We had passed several fortune-tellers' stalls, including Gypsy Rose Lee's and Madam Petulengro's, but now Ben stopped outside Gypsy Ethelinda Zima's garish booth. The hoarding said: 'Cross Gypsy Zima's palm with silver and she will lift the vail (sic) on your future. The hand is the MIRROR OF THE SOUL. Palmist to the stars. 1/- per consultation.' There were indeed photographs of a number of stars of stage and screen (and telly) pictured on the display but whether any of them had ever set foot in the booth wasn't clear.

A shilling was a good deal cheaper than what some of the more famous names were charging and for a while we dared each other to go in. In the end, we decided to go in together.

'One at a time,' said a bouncer with an earring and a colourful scarf on his head.

'We're only small,' Ben said.

'None of your lip, sunshine,' the bouncer said, 'or you'll get the back of my hand. One at a time or not at all. Which is it to be?'

'You go,' I said.

'No, you go,' he said.

'Fuck's sake,' said the bouncer.

'All right, me then,' Ben said and he held up a shilling.

'You pays 'er inside,' the bouncer said, lifting a heavy curtain for Ben to go in.

He was in there for about ten minutes while I watched the trams, single deckers and double deckers, clanging away to Star Gate in the South and Bispham in the North. I think in those days you could even get to Fleetwood. Perhaps you still can.

I was obsessed with trams. They'd been abandoned in Blackburn in 1949, the year I was born. I blamed the council. I still do.

When Ben emerged, he looked thoughtful.

'Right, here goes,' I said.

'Put your money away,' Ben said. 'It's a load of cobblers.'

'What did she say?' I asked.

'Well, there was the "cross my palm with silver" lark and then she looked at my hands. She said that my life line was long but cloudy at the end, whatever the flipping 'eck that means. Then she said, this is your heart line. It's broken in several places so you are going to have a rocky love life. She asked me if I had a girlfriend and I said I had dozens.'

'No, you haven't,' I said.

'I know, but she doesn't know that, does she?'

'Go on,' I said.

'She said, "this is your head line. You're obviously very intelligent".'

'Well, that's a bucket of tripe for a start,' I said.

'Eff off,' Ben said. 'Then she looked in her poncey crystal ball and said: "Things are not going to be easy for you, child, and very soon your life is going to be turned upside down - but be brave. One day you are going to set the world on fire."'

'Do you believe her?' I said.

'Do I 'eck as like,' he replied.

5.   PLEASURE BEACH

'COME ON. LET'S GO TO THE PLEASURE BEACH,' I said.

This was probably the one thing we had been looking forward to most all day. The name is a bit confusing because it's really a fun fair and it's not actually on the beach. I suppose nowadays it would look a bit tame compared with the white knuckle rides at the likes of Flamingo Land or Alton Towers.

Of course, there was always an Easter Fair in Blackburn's outdoor market place and there were some good rides. I liked The Caterpillar which was at the King William Street end of the fair, if I remember rightly. It went round and round and up and down and then, after a few circuits, a green canvas cover would slowly unfurl over the carriages so that from outside it looked like a giant caterpillar going crazily round and round with a humping movement, while inside teenagers giggled and snogged and groped in the green semi-dark. We were still a bit young for all that, of course.

There were the Bumping Cars at the Victoria Street end, but if you walked up past the carpet shop and the milliner's towards Booths, where the fruit and veg stalls usually were, the biggest attraction was probably the Big Wheel. The wildest thrill was when your car stopped at the top for a while and you could see right across the fair. Night time was best with all the coloured lights. Teddy boys would rock the cars as they went up the wheel but I wasn't up for that.

The Pleasure Beach at Blackpool was in a different league. We were dying to try the Big Dipper which was at the back of the site. It was world-famous in those days - that's what the publicity said anyway. The frame on which the tracks were built was massive and the first long haul as the carriages were winched up to the highest point seemed to take ages. It was certainly high - three big wheels high, perhaps. You could see the Tower ahead of you and loads of terraced houses to the right.

We were lucky enough to be seated right at the front of the carriage. It paused at the top for a few dizzying moments and then seemed almost to fall into the first dip. It was near vertical and the acceleration was so dramatic it made your balls tighten. The impetus was enough to take you to a peak nearly as high, then round a bend so that Blackpool Airport was ahead and below, and down again and up, to ever decreasing heights and gentler slopes.

At last we coasted into the final runway.

'That were bloody champion!' Ben said. 'I reckon we should do it again, don't you?'

'Yeah,' I said. 'Shame not to.'

So we paid the man and did it again.

Then we went on the log flume and got wet, so we had a hot dog while we dried off.

'They always smell better than they taste,' I said.

'I know,' Ben said. 'The bread's like cotton wool.'

'And they never give you enough onions,' I said.

'They make the sausages out of pigs' dicks, you know,' Ben said.

'They do not, you soft get,' I said. 'You don't half tell some whoppers. Come on, let's go on the Bumping Cars.'

We could have shared but decided it was worth the expense to have a car each. It wasn't long before Ben got a telling off. He'd been chasing me and bashing into me, and then zig-zagged and disappeared until he was suddenly coming towards me and hit me head on, and a shower of sparks crackled at the top of his contact pole.

Then he turned his attention to a couple of girls in a pink car, trapping them in a corner and repeatedly ramming them as they screamed, whether in agony or ecstasy it was hard to tell.

An attendant dressed in a cowboy outfit came swinging over to Ben across the arena, standing on the buffers of other cars and holding on to the contact poles until he reached him. I slid my car alongside to hear what was going on.

'Back off and let them out!' the man shouted.

'They're enjoying it,' Ben replied.

'No, they're not,' the man said. 'They've paid their money like everybody else and you're wasting it for them. Now, back off or I'll throw you out so fast your arse'll burst into flames. DO IT!'

Pulling his best hatred face, Ben swung the nose of his car aside and the girls edged out and joined the circling traffic.

'Now,' the man said, 'you go round in one direction and stop being a wazzock, or you're out of here. Got it?'

'What's the point of calling them Bumping Cars if you're not allowed to bump?' Ben shouted. I could see that he was getting dangerously angry.

'They're not called Bumping Cars for a start,' the man said. 'They're called Dodgems. Only kids call them Bumping Cars.'

'I *am* a kid!' Ben protested and put his foot down, shooting off into the arena. The little red car had a giant squid painted on its nose and I noticed, what I'd missed before, that it was called *Captain Nemo*.

Ben did half a circuit and then turned the car a hundred and eighty degrees into the oncoming traffic. I could see even at a distance that he was fuming. He faced the mass of vehicles and started bashing cars left, right and centre.

I looked back to the man who had bollocked Ben. He was gesturing towards the control booth with one hand and pointing at Ben with the other.

Suddenly, Ben's car went dead and the traffic flowed around him. The man jumped into an empty car in the line by the buffers, went out to Ben's stranded vehicle, shunted him to the side, pulled him out by his ear and shouted right into his face. I saw Ben trying to kick his shins but the man pushed him away. Ben went reeling but managed to stay on his feet.

I abandoned my car (dark green, jungle leaves, *Dr Livingstone*) and ran round the decking to catch up with my friend.

'He's mental, he is,' Ben was shouting. 'He's a complete spaz. Oy, you, Lone Bloody Ranger! I hope your rabbit dies and you can't sell the hutch!'

But the man wasn't paying him the slightest bit of attention.

Ben tried to sulk but couldn't keep it up once we were in the Hall of Mirrors. There was a fat Ben, a thin Ben, Ben like an hourglass, Ben with a squashed and elongated head, Ben with huge biceps, and a dwarf Ben with enormous feet. I bent him into outrageous positions in front of the distorting mirrors and we went into hysterics.

When we came out, the sun was shining cheerily and the wind had dropped, so that it was impossible to believe that we had arrived in a gale that morning. But time was getting on.

'We'd better be heading back,' Ben said.

'No, we have to try this first,' I said.

We were standing outside The Haunted Swing.

'We haven't got time,' Ben said.

'Yeah, we have,' I said. 'We can go back in a tram. It'll take no time.'

'You and your trams,' Ben said.

He pronounced it 'ter-rrams.'

'Stewpot loves his ter-rrams!' he sang.

'Shurrup, and come on,' I said.

The sign had a picture of a ghost on a swing. It was the kind of ghost you might see in *The Beano*. It read:

The Haunted Swing
The Gravity of the Situation!

'What does it do?' Ben said.

'I don't know, do I?' I said. 'Come on!'

Despite the improvement in the weather, we appeared to be the only punters. We were shown into a spooky room and placed on a settle covered with brocade, and a girl with a squint made a lot of fuss about making sure we'd fastened our seat belts properly.

She went out and closed the door. The room was wood-panelled with framed portraits on the wall. A fire burncd in thc gratc framed by a carved fireplace. There were two candelabra on a sideboard and the candles were lit. They were fake of course and, looking back, the whole thing was like the painted set of a corny amateur dramatic production. But it was spooky all right - and we sat in silence, afraid to speak.

There was a crack and then a creaking noise and the seat began, ever so slowly, to revolve. When it had turned forty-five degrees and we were lying on our backs, looking up at the ceiling, the machinery stopped, and we lay there in a silence which was spookier than any sound effects might have been.

Another crack, and we creaked another forty-five degrees and stopped. We were upside down. The fire continued to burn and did not fall out of the grate. The candles continued to burn, though the flames didn't bend and continued to point downwards. Ben grabbed my wrist and held it very tightly.

We turned again and now we were looking face down at the shabby carpet.

'Oh Jesus,' Ben said. 'Oh Jesus. Jesus, Jesus, Jesus.'

Another turn and we were back where we started, and Ben was fiddling with his seat belt as if to get out when the swing began to turn again, slowly at first. It did the whole three hundred and sixty degrees, without stopping this time - and again, and again, gathering speed all the time, till the features of the room were just a blur.

'Oh, fuck!' Ben cried. 'Oh, fuck! Oh, fuckity-fuckity-fuck-fuck!'

Eventually, it slowed down and came to a halt; harsh lights came on from somewhere, and a door, opposite the one by which we had entered, sprang open. We unbuckled and spilled out on to the sunny path.

Ben looked green.

'Are you all right?' I said.

'I thought I were going to be sick. I don't know what you're laughing at.'

'There's one thing though,' I said.

'What's that?' he said, bending over with his hands on his knees and taking deep breaths. 'What are you on about?'

'Well, you know that gypsy woman?'

'Yeah. What about her?'

'Well, she said your life were going to turn upside-down, didn't she?'

6.   CIRCUS

'YAH!' BEN SAID. 'Coincidence.'

'Oh, yeah,' I said. 'Why are you looking so freaked out then?'

'That ride. If I'd thrown up, it would have gone over everything, including you, so I don't know what you're laughing at, you div.'

'You're the div. I'm laughing at you, divvy, 'cos that ride's a con.'

'You what?' Ben said. 'How do you make that out?'

'We weren't moving at all. It was the room that was revolving. It's an optical illusion.'

'Bollocks!'

'It isn't "bollocks". Did you feel any strain on your seat belt when we were upside down?'

Ben pulled a 'you might have a point' face.

'And when we were facing the floor? Your whole weight would be straining against the straps, wouldn't it?'

Ben nodded reluctantly.

'But why did I feel sick?'

'Because your eyes told your brain that you were spinning round and your brain told your belly and your belly wanted to throw up.'

'Bloody hell fire,' Ben said. 'That's clever.'

'You know when you're sitting on a train and the train next to you moves off and you think it's you that's moving. It's like that.'

'I get you,' Ben said.

'And another thing,' I continued. 'I noticed some fag ends in a corner. When the ride started, they slid along and then dropped - on to the ceiling, then the other wall, and then back on to the floor.'

'Woo, smartypants!' Ben said.

'You could say that.'

'Right then Sherlock Holmes, we'd better get that ter-rrram.'

I'd once been to Blackpool with Mum and Dad during the Illuminations and that's when I fell in love with trams. Some of the trams were decorated with coloured lights to resemble other kinds of transport. I remember a steam train with a fat funnel and a cow-catcher, a battleship, a paddle steamer and a sky rock-et. They were totally magical.

Even the everyday tram we caught from the Pleas-ure Beach to the Tower was magic, partly because it was a double-decker with green and cream livery. We scrambled up the spiral stair to the top deck and the front seats were free. I was in raptures as the tram clanged along, stopping frequently.

'Stewpot loves his ter-rrams!' Ben sang out as new passengers appeared at the top of the stairs and found seats. He was kneeling on the seat and facing down the length of the deck. 'Stewpot loves his ter-rrams!'

I moved to the seat on the other side of the aisle and turned to the other passengers.

'I'm not with him, you know,' I said. 'Never seen him in my life before.'

At the entrance to the Tower Menagerie, Mr Butterfield was handing out tickets.

'Now you need to look after your tickets carefully, boys, because they're for the zoo *and* the circus. For heaven's sake, don't throw them away once we get into the zoo or you won't get into the circus later. One at a time, please, one at a time. No, not you.'

Mr Butterfield pushed away Nigel Clitheroe's questing hand.

'I'll look after your ticket, Nigel. We don't want a repeat of last time.'

We all knew what he was talking about. The Butterfields had taken us to see the pantomime at the Palace Theatre in January - *Aladdin*, I think it was. Mr B handed out the tickets on the Boulevard just outside the theatre doors. Somehow, Nigel managed to lose his between there and the foyer - a distance of no more than five yards. He was made to turn out his pockets and the rest of us scoured the area, but it had vanished.

That boy was a mess.

I don't remember much about the menagerie except that it stank. You know how foul the scent of cat piss is: this was *big* cat piss. There was a male lion with a magnificent mane. He was pacing backwards and forwards listlessly. The muscles under his sandy coat were terrifying. He whisked his tail with its darker tassel backwards and forwards across his rear legs. Ben tried pulling faces at him. The lion turned his head to look at him, gave a low growl, lifted his tail and squirted out a horizontal stream of steaming piss as if in contempt. There were tigers, magnificent tigers, also pacing from side to side. I couldn't get over how big they were.

The big cats are what stick in my memory, but there were also bears and monkeys, and a dingo and hideous, creepy, spotted hyenas. There were crocodiles and turtles in the reptile house, and in the aviary there were brilliantly coloured birds which hooted and screeched and whistled like some kind of manic alarm system that had gone out of control.

On the whole I thought the zoo was a sad kind of place. The animals, even the big ones, were kept in rows of concrete prisons with iron grilles on the viewing side. Some of the animals were asleep. Only the chimps seemed happy to be watched, and showed off like toddlers do.

The elephant enclosure was empty and there was a notice saying that they were being prepared for their performance in the circus. It said that they were often walked on the sands and enjoyed a splash about in the sea. I would have paid good money to see that. There was a photograph of one of them standing in the shallows with the tower in the background.

I was getting a bit bored by now so I was glad when Mr B ushered us towards the entrance to the circus. The arena was huge but we had good seats near the front and had whipped ourselves into a state of hyper-excitement, fuelled, no doubt, by all the sweets, junk food and fizzy drinks we had been consuming all day.

The auditorium lights dimmed, coloured spotlights travelled around the arena, the orchestra struck up, brash and brassy:

YA ta tiddle tiddle
YA ta dada

- and the ring master ran on with his red coat and riding boots. He whipped off his shiny top hat and extended his arms, hat in one hand and whip in the other, and saluted the audience. The audience went wild.

The orchestra segued into the *William Tell Overture* and plumed horses came on and galloped round in a circle and girls with sequins and long legs did acrobatics on their backs. The ring master cracked his whip and the horses went in the opposite direction and soon there were two circles of horses, one galloping clockwise and another inner circle going anti-clockwise and - so what?

Ben yawned beside me.

The truth is that it was all a bit of an anti-climax. After the gruesome business of the 'pregnant boy' and the sex-diseases and the consequences of self-abuse; after the fortune-telling and the intoxicating fairground rides and the revolving room; after the terr-am and even the foul-smelling zoo, it all seemed a bit naff. Whether we were just tired or whether we considered ourselves too old for this stuff, it felt flat.

I didn't find the clowns remotely funny. The horn-tooting when their car collapsed, their over-sized shoes, the custard pies, the pratfalls - it all seemed a bit banal and childish. When one of them came staggering to the ringside with a bucket of water on a pole and tripped, I knew somehow that the bucket had been fixed and that it didn't contain water but silver confetti. The littl'uns in the front rows squealed with delight as it came shivering over them and, yes, I thought, that's about the right level.

The elephants lumbered on and the orchestra played *Nellie the Elephant* with a tuba *ostinato* and enthusiastic flourishes from the trombonist. Inevitably, they trooped round in a circle, with each elephant holding the tail of the elephant in front with his trunk.

I like elephants and I thought all this was undignified. They wore plumes like the horses and it was like a parody of a more agile animal. I know that this is a mainstream view now and that most circuses don't have animals at all these days ,but it wasn't mainstream at the time. I felt so sad when these majestic beasts were made to sit up and beg by a little creep in a turban holding a hooked stick. I wanted one of the elephants to pick him up and hurl him into the air.

It wasn't that I didn't appreciate the skills involved in many of the acts. I could understand the oohs and aahs from the audience as glittering youngsters, leapt and swung from trapeze to trapeze, somersaulting in the air. There was a hushed silence in the crowd as a lad wearing nothing but a pair of silver tights made his way along the high wire, balancing on one slippered foot, while the other foot tested backwards and forwards until it came down on the wire and took his weight. His long balancing pole had a green light at one end and a red one at the other like an aeroplane. A ghoulish voice-over pointed out that Arturo Mirabile scorned a safety net - one false move and he would crash to certain death.

Of course I admired Arturo's courage but I also wondered if it was worth the crick in my neck which was the result of my staring upwards for so long. I was aware that Ben had disappeared from my peripheral vision and turned to find him fast asleep, his feet on the back of the seat in front.

Things bucked up a bit when a cage was rapidly thrown up around the inside of the ring. Parts of it were flown in from above and others came from the tunnel. Workers ran around locking the structure together. The speed with which they completed the cage was almost an act in itself.

The lions ran in from the tunnel snarling and roaring and I have to admit that this was quite a spectacle. They leapt up on to platforms around the edges of the cage and clawed at the air as the trainer thrust a chair at them. But there was not much more to it than that except when the trainer put his head briefly in the mouth of a great beast with a huge mane. When it became clear that he was not going to get his head bitten off, my interest waned rapidly.

When jugglers came in on unicycles, I slumped into the same semi-horizontal position as Ben. No matter how many sparkly balls or juggling clubs they had in the air at a time or plates whirling on poles; no matter how expertly they managed the cycles, jockeying backwards and forwards for balance, or even spinning on the spot, it all left me cold.

Suddenly, the lights dimmed. The ring master ran on in a follow spot and proclaimed: 'My lords, ladies and gentlemen, it is my pride and pleasure to give you: THE MIGHTY PROMETHEUS, LORD OF FIRE!'

Ben sat bolt upright. Riding an impossibly tall unicycle, wearing a red satin leotard exposing a hairy torso, and sporting a black leather helmet with horns, on the tips of which were flames, came the Mighty Prometheus, juggling fire sticks. This was more like it.

He did several circuits of the ring, whirling the sticks, aflame at both ends, and tossing them high, leaving traceries of hot light in the semi-darkness. Coming to the middle of the ring again, he tossed the sticks to an assistant, one by one, and she extinguished them in a bucket.

Now another assistant ran to him holding torches, three in each hand, and, one by one, he extinguished them in his mouth.

'Hell's bells!' Ben whispered beside me.

The best was yet to come. Prometheus was handed a flaming baton and used it to light his breath. As he cycled round, pedalling and back-pedalling, there would be a roll of drums, a shimmering of cymbals and then a great crash from a gong, and he would breathe out a rolling tongue of yellow flame, to wild applause.

Then the lights went out completely. There was silence even though the auditorium was full of kids. The darkness was charged with suspense. Then - quietly at first but growing, the drums, the cymbals, and with the gong a great blare of trumpets - a plume of dazzling fire, twenty feet high, roared into the air, illuminating the upturned face of the Mighty Prometheus himself.

The audience were on their feet, applauding, shouting, stamping and whistling.

'Bloody hell fire!' Ben said.

7.   FIREWORK

'DID YOU SEE THAT?' Ben said on the train. 'Did you chuffing see that?'

'What?'

'The fire-breather. Prometheus. It were just incredible.'

We had a compartment to ourselves. I was feeling really tired and just wanted to snuggle down and snooze, but Ben was still buzzing with excitement.

'I could do that,' he said.

'Don't be a bigger cloth-head than God made you,' I replied. 'You'd kill yourself.'

'I know how they do it.'

'No you don't.'

'I do an' all. I read about it in the Library down town.'

'Go on then, if you're so clever, how do they do it?'

'Well, they don't actually breathe fire,' he said. 'I mean, they don't actually have fire in their mouths.'

'Yeah, well I never thought they did.'

'Just checking. You can never tell with you. Sometimes you seem right clever but, most of the time, you're just thick as a brick.'

I let it ride.

'Anyway,' he said. 'Here's what you do. You take a big mouthful of paraffin or some special stuff that's like it. You have to be careful not to swallow it or breathe it in because it's toxic. And then, you need your ignition source, a torch or a lighter. Prometheus would have had his helpers making sure that everything was ready for the crucial moment, passing up the fuel and concealing the light, then woosh! Are you listening, Stewpot?'

He gave me a sharp jab in the ribs with his elbow.

'The secret is in the breathing,' he went on. 'Obviously, you have to be dead careful not to breathe back the flame or it will scorch your mouth and your throat and your lungs, and it could even be fatal.

'What you want is total breath control. You want to expel the fuel into the ignition in a fine mist, at an even speed, with as much power behind it as possible. I'll bet the Great Prometheus does breathing exercises all day and every day. I'll bet he practises with water, again and again and again, getting that jet of mist just right. Are you listening, you dozy git?'

I was and I wasn't. I was so tired my head kept sinking on to my chest.

'That's what I'm going to do when I grow up. I'm going to be a firebreather.'

'*If* you grow up,' I mumbled.

'I'll call myself the Brookhouse Dragon.'

'Very nice, but I wouldn't recommend it.'

'Why not?'

'Well, the firework up your bum didn't turn out too well, did it?'

If he answered, I didn't hear it. I had slipped helplessly into a comfortable sleep, though I was still dimly aware of the persistent rhythm of the train going over the sleepers.

Ta dadada Ta dadada - the train said.

When it pulled into Blackburn Station, with a squeal of brakes and great belches of steam, it was Ben who was asleep on my shoulder and who had to be shaken till he woke up, dazed and disorientated.

The Alarming Incident of the Firework up the Bum was really preceded by *The Incident of the Ignition of the Fart*.

Ben was a smoker. Everybody knew it, even Mr Butterfield.

'You could be a really good singer, Ben,' he'd said. 'I mean a really remarkable singer.'

In my heart of hearts, I knew this was true. I was good but he was so much better and I felt an ugly pang of jealousy.

'But you're not going to make it unless you cut out the fags,' Mr Butterfield continued.

'But I don't smoke, sir.'

'Oh, come on, Ben. I can smell it on you.'

'That'll be from home, sir. Me mum and dad both smoke, sir. Chain smokers, they are, sir. I've told them it's bad for their health but they won't listen to me. The smell of it gets in your clothes and your hair and everything, but what can you do, sir?'

Mr B gave up. Ben was a poor liar but a persistent one. He was a smoker all right and he had a prodigious collection of cigarette lighters.

One crisp October evening, Mr Butterfield was late for choir practice. We were supposed to be rehearsing hymns and an anthem for the All Saints service. We had been playing hide and seek among the gravestones but had grown bored with the game.

Ben leapt up on to a great big oblong of a gravestone about three feet high. It probably belonged to some distinguished Victorian elder of the borough. It made a perfect stage.

'Who wants to see me light a fart?'

'Me!' we cried.

'I had cheese pie and baked beans for dinner,' Ben announced, 'so this one is going to be a right stinker. Come up here, you.'

He gestured to Kenneth Buck (the red-haired skinny dipper) to join him on his improvised stage. Kenny leapt up and bowed to the audience.

'You see before you,' Ben announced, 'the one and only, Mighty Bumblaster, and his assistant, Scarlet Ken!'

They bowed extravagantly and blew kisses to their audience of ten choristers and two probationers. We applauded like lunatics.

'Behold!' Ben said, and produced from his pocket a bright red Bic cigarette lighter. He held it out between finger and thumb and showed it round like a conjurer displaying a playing card. With a flourish he handed it to Kenny, dropped his trousers, displaying baggy white Y-fronts, and bent over, sideways on to us.

'Scarlet Ken,' he cried theatrically. 'Ignite the flame!'

Kenny did so.

'Silence, please!' Ben cried. 'Scarlet Ken, apply the flame!'

Kenny applied the flame to Ben's bottom and Ben let loose a protracted rip-roaring fart.

WOOF! - the detonation was surprisingly loud as a bright green flame boomed into the dark October night.

Ben hitched up his trousers and bowed to massive applause. Kenny pretended to pass out and then propped himself up on his elbows.

'Faugh! What you got up there? A dead rat?' he said.

We were still whooping and whistling when Mr Butterfield came round the corner.

'What are you boys up to?' he said.

'Nothing, sir,' we chanted in unison.

'Come in then, out of the cold.'

A few minutes later we were singing

Who are these like stars appearing,
These, before God's throne who stand?

- with expressions of innocence the angels might have envied.

As I said, this exploit was but the prelude to *The Alarming Incident of the Firework up the Bum*. Drunk on the applause he had earned for his fire-breathing bottom, Ben decided to go one further.

Bonfire Night was fast approaching with all its excitements: the bonfire itself with its leaping flames and sparks rising through the smoke into a black sky; the sharp, acrid smell of sulphur and cordite; the whizzing, banging and whistling of fireworks; showers of coloured sparks rushing into the air; whirling Catherine Wheels fizzing as they spun; rockets exploding in a coloured death high in the sky; treacle toffee and potatoes baked in the embers of the fire.

I still have a mental picture of Ben staring into the heart of the bonfire transfigured by the light, his eyes round as saucers, unblinking, bewitched.

The time between Bonfire Night and Christmastime was a bit of an anticlimax for us boys, especially since the Christmas frenzy didn't start as early then as it does nowadays. It rained for much of November and the rain turned to sleet. We yearned for proper snow but it didn't happen. School exams loomed on the horizon.

What kept us going was the fact that Ben had promised us a special stunt. He had saved a firework called a Golden Fountain from Bonfire Night, and was going to stick it up his bottom and light it. He said he just needed a dry night to stage his spectacular.

Patience was rewarded one freezing night in December when the air was so clear that the sky was thick with stars. We had decided that St John's graveyard was not an appropriate venue. Normally we didn't have any such scruples but if bums were to be exposed, well, it didn't seem right. Instead the plan was that, after choir practice, we would troop round to the back street behind Ben's house on Brookhouse Lane, where the miracle would be performed by starlight.

Scarlet Ken had been coached in his role and the introduction must have been scripted by Ben because Kenny was really quite thick. Ben must have been watching *The Good Old Days* on television. This was a programme which aimed to reproduce the atmosphere of an Edwardian Music Hall. The audience wore Edwardian costume and enthusiasm was whipped up by the compère who used long words and a lot of alliteration.

Scarlet Ken could not declaim because the houses on either side were close and we didn't want adults to interfere. Instead he employed a melodramatic stage whisper.

'My faithful friends and fine fellow followers of the Mighty Bumblaster! He will this very night from his fundament send out a fantastic fountain of FIRE!'

We applauded vigorously but quietly.

'Behold!' Kenny whispered. He held the firework in one hand and the lighter in the other. He showed them round with the same conjurer's flourishes.

'Behold!'

Ben dropped his trousers and pants to his knees. Our torches played on his bum. It was shockingly white in the darkness.

'Scarlet Ken, the firework!' said the Mighty Bum-blaster. Kenny handed it over. Ben put it between his buttocks and clenched them tight. The firework protruded horizontally.

'Scarlet Ken, light the blue touch paper and retire!'

Kenny did so. For some moments nothing seemed to happen and then, hissing and crackling, a rush of golden rain blazed horizontally out of Ben's bottom.

Forgetting the need to be quiet we clapped wildly.

Then it all went wrong. The Golden Fountain drooped and then dropped to the ground, sending a shower of gold sparks directly at Ben's bare bum.

He let out a yowl, and, clutching the top of his trousers, he shuffled to his own backyard door and let himself in.

'That wasn't meant to happen,' said Scarlet Ken.

8.   HAIRSPRAY

BEN HAD TO BE TAKEN to Casualty. His parents didn't have a car but a neighbour kindly drove him and his mum to the Royal Infirmary. His backside had been peppered with a constellation of tiny burns and there was no question of his sitting down, so he had to kneel beside his mum on the back seat of the car all the way.

His dad had been unsympathetic.

'Serves you right, you silly daft bugger,' he'd said.

'It's not so much the pain,' Ben said later, with a profound sigh. Apparently, he had moved so swiftly as the firework dropped that the burns were not too severe. Despite his fast reflexes, his bottom was studded with little blisters, and the dressings had to be held in place with a pair of plastic knickers.

'Is it that bad?' I asked, genuinely concerned.

'Well, let's just say this,' Ben said. 'I have to eat standing up at the table and I have to sleep lying on my belly. No, what gets me is the humiliation. Mum must have told the whole of Brookhouse what happened. Dad will have told the Landlord in the Whalley Range and he'll have told all the customers. I mean, everybody's really nice and all that. They're agate: "Heard about your accident, cock. Are y'all right? Healing nicely, is it?" And I'm agate: "Yeah, it's nowt really. Thanks for asking" - 'cos I'm polite.

'But I *know*, Stewpot. I know they're laughing up their sleeves at me. They're wetting themselves behind my back.

'Worst thing was the nurse who looked after me. She were dead sweet. She kept a straight face when I told her what had happened and was ever so gentle, but I bet when she went back to her staff room - or whatever they have - she told all her nursey friends and they all fell about and rolled on the floor, laughing fit to burst.

'She were reet fit an' all.'

'Hey, we're not laughing,' Kenny said, and it was true. On the whole, the gang thought it was heroic rather than comic though privately I thought it was a bit of both.

Ben and I lived on the same street and, for years, our lives ran in tandem. Our playground was the network of streets and back streets that ran parallel to one another, streets of two-up-two-down houses with a scrap of a back yard, often with no indoor lavatory or bathroom. Sometimes, we played with Tom Catlow's gang down the Bottom, the cobbled street that ran alongside the smelly River Blakewater and the Brookhouse Mill on the other side. We'd play football and street cricket or rounders, or games such as 'British bulldog'; 'Please, sir, may I cross the water?'; 'Delavio'; 'The big ship sails through the alley-alley-oh'; 'Mother, may I?', and 'What's the time Mr Wolf?' - most of them variants on 'Tag' or 'Hide and seek'.

Tommy Catlow gained a place at the grammar school at the same time Ben and I did and we were good friends. He had become famous the previous autumn and was in the papers. His dog had discovered a human skeleton on a demolition site up Larkhill while they were gathering wood for their bonfire. It was the talk of the school for ages and then it sort of blew over.

He was quite a lad. He'd climbed up the inside of the chimney of a disused factory in Little Harwood for a dare. Later on we were to become good friends.

Anyway, Ben and I always used to walk home from school together to Brookhouse Lane. His house was first and I used to drop off there for a bit to play before going home. Both Ben's parents worked so we could get up to mischief until they returned at tea time. Before that were chores.

Ben had a sister called Sandra who was a year younger. Ben's job was to lay and light the fire; Sandra's was to wash up the breakfast pots and to scour any pans that had been left to soak after the previous evening's tea. Ben executed his task in the same priestly way as Canon Balderstone celebrated the Eucharist at St John's, that is, with a good deal of ritual. First he swept out the grey ash from the grate, reserving any clinker. Then he made coils of newspaper, twisting the pages and knotting them. Next we went into the backyard where he chopped wood on the back step with an ancient axe.

Back inside he laid the fire: paper first, then a pyramid of kindling, a wigwam of bigger sticks and just a few dots of coal. Then he would light the paper and we would kneel and watch as it blackened and charred, and yellow flames wrapped around the wood, which spat and crackled until the coal began to glow. Gradually he would add any clinker and then more coal until a happy fire was burning in the grate, with the occasional blue or green flame leaping among the yellow, from the minerals in the coal.

If the fire was not drawing to his satisfaction, he would sometimes stretch a sheet of newspaper across the fireplace with a gap at the bottom. The updraught would encourage a reluctant flicker into roaring yellow flames which you could see through the paper. Sometimes it would begin to go brown in the middle and a black charred circle would appear and the paper would burst into flame, and we would push the floating inferno into the chimney with poker and tongs, rather than let it rush into the room. The fireball would shoot up the chimney, and we would dash outside to make sure it was not on fire.

I never knew Ben's fire fail to 'catch'. Sometimes, if we were running late, through dawdling in Corporation Park on our walk home from school, Ben would use a fire lighter. One would be enough to start the fire without careful tending. Once, as an 'experiment', Ben used four fire lighters. In less than a minute the whole firebox was a dazzling inferno with roaring flames leaping up the flue. Ben watched the spectacle, wide-eyed with the unblinking, mesmerised gaze I'd seen at the circus and then at the bonfire.

Suddenly, he leapt back to reality.

'Oh bugger,' he said, 'that's going to set the chimney on fire.'

We rushed out. The whole street was not ablaze as we'd feared but there *were* clouds of black smoke coming from Ben's chimney, and I thought I saw sparks.

We waited in suspense for several minutes until the smoke turned to a more usual dull grey and we trooped back indoors. The fire was still high but not threatening. All the same, Ben damped it down a bit with some slack. Soon there was a tarry smell and a plume of smoke rose through the slack to show that the fire underneath was still healthy.

Ben and Sandra were always bickering. Anything could trigger it though it was usually Ben who started things. Even though we were at an age when most girls were irritating, I thought Ben often went too far. The provocation was usually verbal and - so it seemed to me at least - nothing to get upset about, but Ben would be relentless: about the braces on her teeth, the fact that her hair sprang back into tight little curls no matter how much she tried to straighten it, or most incendiary of all - the fact that she fancied Tommy Catlow.

'Gimme some of your chocolate,' Ben might say.

'No,' Sandra would reply. 'Buy your own.'

'I'm broke.'

'Well, that's your lookout. Tough cheese.'

'I'll tell Tom you're mad about him.'

'No, you won't.'

'I bloody will if you don't give me some chocolate.'

'Get lost.'

'Not that you stand a chance. He says you look like a camel's arse.'

'No, he doesn't.'

'Oh yes he does,' Ben would say. 'He says he'd rather *kiss* a camel's arse than look at your mardy face.'

These spats usually ended in tears. Or Sandra would fly at him in a rage, fists flailing. Ben would hold her at arm's length with one hand and give her little slaps about the face with the other.

This embarrassed me - no, I'll go further, it distressed me - though Ben was only a year older than Sandra, he was bigger and stronger, and besides, my parents had drummed into me that it was never ever excusable to hit a female. Usually I did nothing - because I was a guest in their house and because Ben was my friend.

There was one occasion, though, when I couldn't watch the bullying any more. They'd been squabbling as usual and now Ben was sitting on his sister with his knees on her upper arms. He was turning her head from side to side by the ears. I couldn't watch this and pulled him off her and to his feet. We stood with our faces close to each other and I had my hand on his shoulder. I told him that if he carried on behaving like this we couldn't be friends any longer.

He shrugged my hand away roughly and without saying a word, returned to building the fire he'd barely started before the squabble erupted. There was plenty of wood indoors so he hadn't needed to go out to chop more. Consequently, he hadn't yet taken the ash to the bin.

As the fire 'took' and the wood began to crackle, he sat back on his haunches, looked at me and grinned. Then he sprang to his feet and picked up the ash pan. He went into the kitchen, and through the open door I could see him tip the ash into Sandra's washing up water. Sandra let out a wail.

Ben came back, closing the door behind him, re-placed the pan under the grate and sat on the hearth rug, grinning at me again.

'That was a dirty trick,' I said.

He shrugged his shoulders.

'Yeah, well,' he said. 'Are we playing pontoon or not?'

'You're a bastard sometimes. Do you know that?' I said.

'You can be 'Bank' if you want,' he said, standing up and picking up a pack of cards from the mantel-piece.

We began to play, kneeling on either side of a stained coffee table.

There was no sound from the kitchen. I could only suppose Sandra had had to start all over again.

After a few rounds where Ben scored pontoon twice and I began to suspect him of cheating, but I couldn't see how, he threw down his cards.

'This is boring,' he said. 'Hang on.'

He went to a cupboard in the corner with a sliding door. It was actually the glory hole under the stairs. He emerged after a moment with an aerosol of V05 hairspray, presumably his mum's.

'Watch this,' he said, and sent a blast of hairspray directly into the fire.

The fire blazed up with a roar. It was like magic.

'Ben, stop it,' I cried. 'That's bloody dangerous.'

He did it again.

'It could kick back and explode the bleeding can,' I said.

'Bollocks!' Ben said.

He did it again. And again.

Just then the kitchen door opened and Sandra came in, carrying the plastic washing up bowl. She walked steadily, the water slopping about a bit, until she reached us and then, in one movement, she tipped the dirty water over the fire. With a hiss of steam, it went out.

Ben's face was suffused with rage.

And then suddenly he began to laugh.

'Game, set and match to Miss Westwell,' he shouted.

And all three of us began to laugh.

There was something I didn't like about Ben's laugh, though.

It was maniacal.

9.   CONVALESCENCE

BEN AND I HAD BEEN FRIENDS for as long as I could remember.

'They're like twins, them two,' my mother would say to her friends in the Co-op.

'Siamese twins more like,' Mrs Haydock from the top end would say.

'Joined at the hip,' Mum would say. 'Inseparable like. Mind you, they're allus up to mischief.'

'But they're not bad lads, though, are they?' Mrs Kenyon would chime in.

I would be dying of embarrassment.

'Come on, mum,' I would plead. I'd only accompanied her to help carry the groceries. 'I'll miss *Crackerjack*.'

'He's a bonny lad, your Stuart,' Mrs Haydock would say, ruffling my hair as I blushed crimson.

'And so is that Ben,' Mrs Kenyon would say. 'See them together and you really would think they were twin brothers.'

'Like two peas in a pod,' Mrs Haydock would say.

'Aw, come *on*, Mum!' I would whine, tugging at her coat sleeve.

Actually, I don't think we did look very much like each other. We were about the same height, it's true, and he had the same untidy sprawl of hair, my hair was sort of mousy and Ben's was bright blond. Beyond that - well, I couldn't see it.

It was true that we did everything together. When we were very small there'd be sleep overs alternating between Ben's house and mine. I would go to Ben's on a Saturday night and we would be put to bed together in his parents' double bed. Ben's parents would stay at home and the system meant that mine could have a Saturday night out without worrying about me.

A chair under the bedclothes and the bed would become a teepee, an igloo, the cockpit of a fighter plane or a secret underground chamber. Eventually, we would tire of the game and fall asleep wrapped in each other's arms.

When my parents returned, Dad would come and collect me, gently untangling me from Ben. I would sometimes be half-woken and smell the sweet-sour tang of alcohol on his breath. He would carry me across the street and back to my own bed.

The following weekend, we would do it all in re-verse so that Ben's mum and dad could go out. We would be put in my parents' bed and Sandra would have my room. There was a suggestion once that there was plenty of room in the big double for Sandra too and that it would be warmer for her, but Ben wouldn't have it and threatened to scream the house down.

When I was five, I was very ill. I can't remember what it was, measles perhaps. I had to convalesce for a few weeks and Dad moved my bed downstairs and set it up by the window in the front room. For most people in the street (and anywhere in the North, I expect) the front room was the best room, kept in an immaculate state and only used on high days and holidays such as Christmas.

This convalescence really did happen around Christmas-time and I can remember what I received that year: an *Uncle Mac Children's Hour Annual*. Uncle Mac was a presenter on the wireless. I can't remember a thing about the show or the book. I just remember opening the parcel as I sat propped up on the pillows of my sick bed.

It snowed that year, though whether it snowed on Christmas Day or not I can't remember, but it was certainly during my convalescence. I had been really ill with a high fever and it was a while before I returned to eating normally. Meanwhile, Mum would bring me 'pobbies', pieces of bread in warm milk or in Bovril, served in a mug. You ate the bread with a spoon and drank off the liquid.

I remember being propped up on pillows and watching my friends playing outside in the snow. There was snowballing, of course. There would be a white snowburst on the dark coat of a retreating back, a white explosion on the top of a head, and, once in a while, a thwack on the window where the flattened missile would stay for a moment and then slither down the glass. The kids made a slide just outside our house. It probably stretched farther up the slope be-cause, by the time my friends came whizzing past my window with a wave, they were moving at quite a lick. They could have made the slide anywhere in Brook-house Lane but I was right chuffed that they'd made it outside my window to cheer me up.

Best of all was Ben jumping up and down outside the window like a jack-in-the-box, with his face close to the pane and, every time he came up, he would be pulling a different face. He made me laugh till it hurt.

Once, he knocked on the window, and wrote 'Rudolph' on it in lipstick, getting the reverse lettering right apart from the 'p'. Then he slowly emerged from below. He had painted his nose red and was holding his gloves on either side of his head like antlers. Mum and I laughed so much that she forgot to scold him when she went outside to chase him away and clean the window.

I don't think I ever felt so secure as I did at that time. Mum was often with me, darning, doing the ironing, or knitting. She was making me a jumper for when I was better. It was red at the top and blue at the bottom, and across the chest was a white band with a musical stave, a treble clef and a few crotchets all in black. I marvelled at her skill. I loved that jumper and insisted on wearing it till it was far too small for me.

There was always a good fire in the room. Coal was expensive but, because I was poorly, Dad would not bank down the fire for the night until I was fast asleep. I would lie in the luxurious twilight created by the fire, watching the shifting shapes on the ceiling thrown by the dancing flames, and I reflect now, so many years later, that not for nothing, in every culture, is the hearth at the heart of the home - and sacred.

Ben couldn't visit me yet because I might still be infectious, but he would breathe on the glass when Mum wasn't looking, and write rude words in the mist, or draw stick figures doing obscene things. If my laughter made Mum turn around, he would rapidly erase what he'd drawn, breathe on the glass again, and write:

Mrs C is Fit

and make her giggle. He was getting really good at mirror writing.

I don't want to sentimentalise our friendship. It was unselfconscious and innocent. It blew hot and cold and sometimes we bickered and fought. We never apologised for anything and the seamless transition back to cordiality was never marked by any event or conversation. It just happened. We never talked about our friendship and its unique bond. It just was. It was a necessary thing like sunrise and sarsaparilla, playing in the park and potato pies.

As we grew up together, our universe revolved around choir, scouts and school.

10.   CHOIR

MY GRANDFATHER'S CLOCK, The Duke of Plaza Toro, Toreador, La Cucaracha, The Very Model of a Modern Major General, Who is Sylvia? - these are some of the songs we sang around the piano in the vestry when it was too cold to rehearse in the church. *Grandfather's Clock* was my favourite because when you got to 'The clock stopped, short, never to go again, when the old man died', there was a crotchet rest after 'stopped' and 'short' which was really dramatic. The staccato effect had to be sharp and the diction crisp. It seems really simple but Mr Butterfield had us do it again and again until it was right.

I have to admit that the *Modern Major General* was a jolly romp as Mr B would play it faster and faster.

I realise now, of course, that though all this seemed like a holiday from rehearsing the psalms in the draughty church, Mr B was being quite cunning. We were being coached unobtrusively in diction, timing, sight-reading, cohesion, breathing, melody and so much more. We still had the psalms and maybe an anthem to learn and practise but it seemed less of a chore than it sometimes did.

The services were what I liked best. There was the exhilaration that every performer feels before his public. The congregation was our audience and the chancel our stage. Sometimes, there were solos and I was thrilled to be chosen from time to time, though I would be bricking myself beforehand, and in a kind of ecstasy once I'd begun. Sometimes there were duets, and Ben and I were thought a natural pairing, my bright timbre complementing his darker, more mellow tone colour.

Then there were the rituals. We were lifted out of the ordinary by our vestments. When we joined, our cassocks were black and pretty threadbare, but a wealthy parishioner paid for new ones, and we were so excited when they arrived. Purple! Fantastic!

We wore Eton collars rather than ruffs and they were not very comfortable, to be honest. Purple bow ties came with the new outfits. My mum washed both my surplice and Ben's too, because his mum went out to work. Come to think of it, she washed his scout shirt too.

I liked the procession behind the silver cross from the vestry to the choir stalls. I liked the change of liturgical colours on the altar front, the pulpit, the lectern and the canon's stole: Green for Trinity, purple for Advent, red for Whitsun and so on. I liked the rituals of the Eucharist, the mixing of water and wine, the consecration, the Greek and the Latin, the psalms, the anthems, the hymns and the descants. I liked the 'otherness' from daily life. The sermons I was less keen on.

Oh, we must have looked angelic with our shiny faces, especially in the soft light of Evensong, as we sang the *Magnificat* and later *Abide with me, fast falls the eventide*. We must have looked as if we belonged on a Christmas card. It would not have been surprising to see Ben, with his mop of golden hair (brushed tidy for once) at the feet of the Virgin in a stained glass window.

But there was a demon inside the cassock.

St John's was an eighteenth-century church and a little unusual inside. The nave was square and there was a substantial gallery on three sides. In those days, congregations were good, but I only ever saw the galleries occupied at Christmas and Easter. I suppose there were so many pews upstairs and down because once upon a time the centre of Blackburn was more heavily populated.

Sometimes Mr Butterfield would have phone calls to make in Canon Balderstone's office before choir practice began, and the gallery was a great place to play hide and seek or tag. We would race up and down along the pews or leap over them to avoid being caught. It wasn't as spooky as our games in the grave-yard but it was warm and dry.

Once, during one of these delays, Ben and I wandered into the vestibule. The rest of the boys were in the vestry, gossiping about the Rovers' game the previous Saturday. Ben tried the little door which led up to the hidden bell but it was locked. The bell rope hung from the centre of the decorated ceiling and was secured to a brass ring. The rope was thick and red; white and blue cords were twisted into its length. A huge maroon and gold tassel hung from the end. Ben walked over to the rope and fingered the tassel. He turned to look at me and smiled. Temptation sparkled in his eyes.

'No, Ben, don't,' I said.

'Just one,' he said.

'No,' I said.

'We can be down the other side of the church be-fore they come out of the vestry. We can say it's a ghost.'

'No.'

'Oh, come on. Just one.'

'No.'

'You're softer than a baby's bum, you are.'

'Get stuffed,' I said. 'Go and tell your mother she wants you.'

It was just as well I'd put him off because we could hear the others chattering as they came out of the vestry and Mr B playing a few chords on the practice piano which had been pulled out of its home under the pulpit stair.

To the left of the sanctuary were ornamental gates, behind which was the organ console with its four manuals or keyboards, its ranks of stops on either side and its funny wooden pedals. Mr Butterfield had what he called his 'driving mirrors' in there. He could see the altar through one, Canon Balderstone's stall through another, and the pulpit through a third. This meant that he could see the progress of the service and bring in the music on cue. It meant he could also see my side of the choir, which was called *decani*. We had to be on our best behaviour, holding our hymn books in the right position so that our heads were upright, opening our mouths wide on vowels, being still when not singing, and helping the littl'uns to find their places in the psalter.

He could not see *cantoris*, Ben's side, because they had their backs to him. Ben sat immediately op-posite me and tried to make me laugh during the sermon by pulling the most ridiculous faces. He once so nearly succeeded that I practically exploded and snot came running down my face. I tried to disguise it as a sneeze, causing Canon Balderstone to turn and look down severely from the pulpit.

Once, Ben even started a game of pontoon with the boys on either side of him. They leaned back so the congregation couldn't see them and Ben dealt them cards which they hid under their surplices. They'd devised hand signals to indicate 'twist', 'stick' and 'bust'. I remember Ben nearly giving me the giggles again when he held up a queen and an ace in one hand and did a victory V sign with the other. He grinned and pulled his tongue out at me across the chancel.

Once, the start of practice was delayed a little because the organ tuner had been there all day and was just finishing. There was a very narrow door just beyond the organ gates. I hadn't noticed the little door before, just taking it to be a panel like the one on the other side of the sanctuary. Now that it stood open, I saw that it had a keyhole in it.

The other boys had gone off to play in the gallery but Ben and I had been watching. Mr B and the tuner went inside the organ and we heard a bit of tapping. When they came out, Mr B sat at the console and played part of a voluntary. Then he slid off the bench and they both went off to the office. Ben and I slipped through the narrow doorway.

Inside the organ was a weird space. Light filtered between the pipes and made a criss-cross pattern on the dusty floor. We could see the tuner's footprints. There were also a few fag ends. Some of the graduated pipes were metal and some were wood. There was a ladder which went up to a platform behind the pipes on a higher tier. For some reason, the two walls without pipes had wood panelling. Perhaps the church had already been functioning before the installation of the organ. That made sense.

Ben pulled out his ten pack of N⁰· 6 and his Zippo lighter, the pride of his collection. I had seen him practise lighting it with a single flick of his wrist. He lit one now.

'Oh, Ben,' I said.

'Don't be mardy.'

'Smoke'll get out between the pipes.'

'If I lit a fire in here, there'd be a hell of a lot of smoke going out between the pipes, I can tell you. If I lit a fire in here, it would go up like I don't know what! I can see it now, blazing - with the organ playing an' all.'

'You're off your chump, you are,' I said.

11.   SCOUTS

IT WAS AS WELL Ben had finished his fag quickly because we slunk out just in time. As the choir began to
gather for practice, Mr Butterfield announced that
now that the organ had been tuned, we might as well
give it a try out and run through the hymns for
Sunday. Mr B had us stand in the chancel where he
could see us all in the driving mirrors, but before he
sat at the console he locked the narrow door.

Ben was standing beside me. We gave each other
horrified looks. Lent was well advanced, the altar cloth
was purple, the stained glass window above the altar
depicted the crucifixion but I'm sure neither of us was
having spiritual thoughts. As we sang *Forty Days and
Forty Nights* and *Lead us, heavenly Father, lead Us*, I
wondered what it would be like to starve to death inside that dusty tomb behind the organ. Perhaps we
wouldn't be found until next time the organ was
tuned, by which time there would just be two little
piles of bones.

Choir practice was on Thursday, cubs and then
later scouts on Tuesday. St John's didn't have a cub

pack so I was enrolled at the age of eight in the Holy Trinity wolf cubs. Holy Trinity was just as near as St John's, if anything even nearer. Of course, Ben was enrolled at about the same time. I still have a photograph of the two of us standing on our doorstep in our new uniforms: green jerseys and caps, khaki shorts, and red scarves. We must have just joined because there are no insignia or activity badges on our jerseys, and our woggles are just plain. Later we both collected quite a lot of badges and competed for trendiest woggle. Actually, looking at it now, we do look rather alike, apart from our different hair colour. We are both standing proudly to attention and Ben is squinting into the sun.

We both rose rapidly up the ranks. Ben had a natural aptitude for the active life and I was something of a strategist and problem solver. We earned the first silver star on our caps at the same time. It symbolised the Tenderfoot wolf cub opening one eye and then the other. I gained my second star before Ben (and thus had my metaphorical eyes wide open) because I had clean fingernails whereas, according to Akela, Ben's neck had the grubbiest tide mark in the North West.

He must have improved his personal hygiene as a result of this criticism because we both became Sixers at the same ceremony. A Sixer had two stripes on his arm and, as the name suggests, he was in charge of five other boys. I was in charge of Green Six and Ben, Red Six.

When we were about eleven, we moved up into the scouts together. I remember the ceremony even now. The scouts came into the church hall where we usually met and formed up in their horseshoe at one end. We formed the usual circle where we did our dib-dib-dib and dob-dob-dobbing with our yellow flag in the middle. The scouts had their green flag and there was also the union flag with its posh tassels. It was all very ceremonious.

Skipper and Akela called us to attention and then our circle opened into a horseshoe facing the scouts' one. (This had taken a lot of rehearsal.) Akela brought Ben and me forward and we gave the two fingered cub salute for the last time (not that one! - it represented the wolf's ears.) And Skipper replied with the three-fingered scout salute, representing the three promises which we'd had to learn and then made publicly. I've forgotten them, but they were to do with good citizenship. We were then received into the troop.

We both took scouting dead seriously. We borrowed *Scouting for Boys* out of the Public Library and devoured it from preface to index.

Anything to do with camp fires grabbed Ben's attention, of course. He couldn't find anything about rubbing two sticks together. He said that was something people came up with the minute boy scouts were mentioned. He reckoned it would definitely work but that the wood would have to be really dry, and that it would take forever.

We did find this, though, which had us rolling about laughing:

> *If coals or wood are difficult to get for making fires at home, don't forget that old boots, which you often find lying about on dust heaps, make very good fuel.*
>
> *You can do a good turn to any poor old woman in wintertime by collecting old boots and giving them to her for firing.*

I suggested we look for old boots to give to Mrs Birtwistle who lived in the bottom house, and would come out on to her doorstep and screech at us: 'What are you doing down here? Go and play up your own end!'

'She *is* an old boot,' Ben said.

In order to be fully incorporated into the troop we had to complete a number of tasks. I have been thumbing through my own battered copy of the book and came across this requirement. To become a First Class Scout we had to:

Lay and light a fire using not more than two matches, and cook a quarter of a pound of flour and two potatoes without cooking utensils.

We must have achieved this, though I have no memory of it.

We were fast learners and once again Ben and I worked our way up the ranks. As older boys left, vacancies arose and there were opportunities for promotion. This time, Ben made the grade before me and was promoted to Patrol Second and then Patrol Leader of Beaver Patrol. I envied him the two stripes on his breast pocket but tried not to show it. I liked the shoulder knot of the Beavers which was purple and green.

Less than two months later, I had my turn and was promoted straight up to Patrol Leader of Fox. Our shoulder knot was red and yellow. A third patrol was called Hound Patrol. They were good lads but they were not fired by the zealous spirit that drove Ben and me, and tended to do less well in competitive events.

This rivalry was to come to a head at our first big camp.

Meanwhile we played games, acquired skills for badges, went out tracking, and learned our knots. The games were sometimes pretty rough. There were ball games, of course, and the inevitable British Bulldogs, and there was a game involving wooden staves. Pairs of boys from one patrol would crouch down holding these walking poles out at ankle level, and the boys from the other patrols had to run over them like hurdles. The thing was that the poles could suddenly be raised. It wasn't at random - there were rules which I can no longer remember - something to do with timing. Anyway, you could be gingerly stepping over them at one moment and involved in Olympic hurdles the next. The risk of a crack on the shin and a nasty bruise was high.

Tracking was great fun. A couple of scouts from each patrol would set off from the den on Trinity Street and aim to get away as far as possible. A quarter of an hour later the rest of us would set out, the object of the exercise being to find them. *Scouting for Boys* has a chapter on tracking which involves bent twigs, animal tracks, boot marks and so on - but we were town boys and our signs were usually chalked arrows, straight, curved or bent at right angles. These could be on the ground, high or low on a wall, on a lamppost or a pillar box. In a bit of waste land, there might be arrows made of little pebbles or sticks. The route might take us down into town past Thwaites's brewery, or beyond the level crossing at Daisyfield to St.Stephen's Rec, or it might go over Higher Audley and down to the canal or even down to Brookhouse, where Ben and I lived, and the River Blakewater.

As for badges, there was an amazing variety of things you could try your hand at. I got a stamp-collecting badge and Ben learnt to knit, ignoring a certain amount of derision from the others. We both got a cookery badge for making some basic dishes and learning a bit about nutrition and kitchen hygiene. I was a keen swimmer and earned my life-saving badge on the second attempt at Belper Street baths. You had to dive for a brick in the deep end, wearing pyjamas for some reason. You had to bring a person 'in difficulties' to the side of the pool, holding him under the arms, and swimming backstroke.

'What should you do if the person struggles?' said the instructor who was putting us through the tests.

'Knock him out,' I said, having been coached in this by Skip, 'because he will recover from that but wouldn't recover from drowning."

'What if it's a lady?'

'Same,' I said, hoping to God I would never have to do any of this.

Skip wanted us all to apply for the First-Aid Badge and learn how to administer the Kiss of Life. I remember the time when Skip brought a training dummy, borrowed from St John's Ambulance, into the school hall. It was female and looked like a fierce lady librarian. Her legs were nothing to write home about and her knees had a tendency to point in impossible directions, but her breasts, under a fair isle tank top, were substantial. She was called Brenda.

There was a lot of speculation about her as Skipper took her out of her box and laid her out on the floor. When he tilted her head back, putting one hand under her neck, holding her nose with the other, and began breathing into her mouth, there were cheers and wolf whistles, not least because those huge tits went up and down as he breathed into her. Then he turned his head away and repeated the sequence.

'I don't think much to his snogging technique. Do you, lads?' Ben said, leering.

Skip did not reply but linked his fingers and started pressing on her breastbone with the heels of his hands, exerting all his force and counting to thirty. It looked pretty violent. He alternated this with more 'kisses'.

We were struck dumb.

'What if it was a bloke?' somebody said.

'Same business,' Skipper said. 'Wouldn't make any difference.'

We all pulled faces at each other.

'It would prickle,' somebody else said.

'It would be like kissing a hedgehog,' Ben said, and we all laughed like loonies.

Skipper ignored him.

'Right, you hidjus rabble,' Skipper said. 'Your turn. Who's first?'

We fell quiet and there was a shuffling of feet.

'She's bloomin' ugly,' somebody said.

'Would you rather practise on each other?' Skip said.

Retching noises.

Ben stepped forward.

'I'll have a go,' he said, and knelt down beside the dummy.

'That's right,' Skip said. 'Turn your head to the side and breathe in through your mouth and then BLOW hard. You want to get as much air into her lungs as you can.'

Then one by one, we gave Brenda the kiss of life.

12   CAMP

THE OTHER CLICHÉ ABOUT BOY SCOUTS (other than that they can often be found rubbing sticks together in the vain hope of creating fire) is that they are principally involved in tying knots.

Well, maybe, but my reef knot is always perfect and you won't catch me breaking my fingernails trying to untie a granny knot. I can still do a sheet bend, for tying two ropes together, and a round turn and two half hitches for tying a rope to a secure object. I've never been sailing or attempted an air-sea rescue so I don't think I've ever had use for a bowline, but your sheepshank - well now.

Recently, I bought a parasol for the garden table. The cord used to raise it is quite long and a lot of surplus cord lies on the table top. It's a bit sad, I know, but I have a very tidy mind, and this irritated me. So, one morning I tied a sheepshank in the cord. This is a knot that temporarily shortens a rope. The thing is, that my fingers tied it from some deep-seated memory, decades after I'd learnt it, with me scarcely looking at it. What's also handy about it is that you can loosen it with a tug when you want to close the parasol up.

What sheep had to do with it I have no idea.

The end purpose of all this tracking, fire-lighting and knot-tying was camp, to which we looked forward with feverish excitement. The prospect was the be-all-and-end-all in our lives for months. Sometime in February, Skipper gave us all a Roneo'd letter announcing a projected camp somewhere in France. Skipper's neat script was in purple ink and you could still smell the spirit on the shiny paper.

I knew that the scout troops at school and up the posher end of town went to camp in foreign parts every year. There were boys in my form who were in the Woodlands troop - up Shear Bank Road, with purple and yellow scarves, if I remember rightly - who never stopped boasting about it. Ben and I had remained loyal to Holy Trinity, even when we moved up to the Grammar School. We were proud of our red scarves. What's more, it was instilled in us that we were the premier troop: Holy Trinity, 3rd Blackburn (1st and 2nd having disbanded long ago), and we had the right to head civic processions past the Town Hall to the Cathedral, and the honour of bearing the union flag.

Now we were going to show the posh buggers that we were on a par with them. On the way home Ben looked crestfallen.

'What's to do, pal?' I said.

'This,' he said, waving the letter about. I suddenly saw that he was close to tears. 'I'll never be allowed to go on this. Me mum has enough trouble giving me money for subs every week.'

Subscriptions were a few pence.

'And me dad is allus moaning about the cost. He said the uniform cost a month's beer money.'

I knew Ben's uniform was second-hand. We all did. His shirt was several shades paler than the dark green ones the rest of us wore, because it had been washed so often. He never said so but I knew he felt it keenly.

In the event, Ben was not the only one whose family wrote in to say that the proposed camp, near Boulogne, was beyond their means. However, Skipper bid us all not to be downcast. He had promised us a camp, and a camp we should have. He was true to his word. We didn't go to Quesques; we went to Tockholes.

Tockholes (pronounced 'Tockus' locally) is a hamlet, a quarter of an hour's drive to the south of Blackburn. I remember a rather snobbish wince at the announcement. How could I hold my head up at school? There are a number of Lancashire towns whose names seem funny, especially to southerners: Oswaldtwistle, Eccles, Bacup, Rawtenstall and, of course, Ramsbottom. Tockus was in the same league. Tockus, mothers would tell their children, was where the treacle mines were.

So, Ben and I kept quiet about it at school though, in the end, we had more fun than if we'd been to some flash camp in the Dordogne with white water rafting and abseiling.

We went to camp in an open lorry, loaned by a friend of Skip's. Our rucksacks, along with supplies, were piled in the back, and we clambered on top of the pile and moved off, cheering and waving to local women who had come out on to their well-scrubbed doorsteps, with curlers under their headscarves, to see us off. We whooped as we came down into Salford and into the centre of town, and people waved back at us. Ken, the assistant scoutmaster, followed us in his mini so that we had emergency transport if necessary, once the lorry driver had gone back to work.

Before long we were in open countryside. Eventually we turned off Rock Lane, down a bumpy track, past a farm whose name I no longer remember, on to our site, an area of rough pasture beyond which was scrub, leading down to a stream - our water supply.

As soon as we'd unloaded the lorry and it drove off, the first thing was to erect a flagpole, securing it with guy ropes. We formed our horseshoe around it, the union jack was run up, we saluted it and reaffirmed the Scout Oath. Before we could even think about our sleeping quarters, we were all involved in putting up an enormous ex-army bell-tent which would be the troop headquarters, quartermaster's stores and first-aid post. Only then did we erect our own tents.

The site actually sloped a little towards the stream. I staked out a reasonably flat patch for Fox Patrol's ridge tent, and Ben created a lodge for his Beavers a little further down and nearer the stream. Hound Patrol pitched their tent on a slope with the end opposite the entrance flap rather lower down. The result was that, after a stormy night, poor Jimmy Griffin was lying in a chilly puddle and the flysheet of their tent had come loose and blown away. It was discovered later in a tree by the stream.

Later, Skipper had to help them find a better site and start again.

In our tent, I declared that my Patrol Second, Dave Forbes, should place his sleeping bag in the draughty station by the entrance flap so that he could alert me in case of attack. I would sleep at the (draught-free) far end so that I could immediately take command in the face of hostilities.

'Very smart, Stewpot,' Ben said when I told him about these arrangements. 'I'm sleeping in the middle, between the twins.'

'Why?' I asked.

'Because it's warmest,' he laughed. 'Got to be some privileges to the burden of command.'

This is where the knots came into play. We roped off our territories. My stave with its fox pennant stood by the entrance. We made a rack for billy cans and our enamel plates and mugs from sticks bound with knots. Ben's enclosure was much the same, though they'd even made a boot scraper from an old knife knotted to wooden supports.

Naturally, Ben's fireplace was smarter than ours. We'd both created surrounds from flat stones found near the stream, but Ben's was a piece of engineering of a higher order. The stones had been sorted according to size and built up rather like a dry stone wall. He'd even foraged a small sheet of corrugated iron which could be moved around to create a back to the fire, directing the prevailing wind into it. Our fire was efficient but a billy can set on Ben's fire would boil sooner.

Growing boys have appetites like lions; boys growing up in the outdoors can eat a lion raw and then come back for the cubs. I have no idea why food cooked and eaten outdoors tastes better but it's true. We lived on spam fritters, rissoles from a packet, corned beef hash, stews which took forever to cook, tinned peaches with evaporated milk, pilchard sandwiches, banana fritters and buttery baked potatoes. Best of all was the smell of frying bacon mingling with wood smoke. We wolfed it down with baked beans and a wodge of white bread slathered with butter, all washed down with a mug of strong tea. Who cared if there was the odd leaf or bit of twig in the brew?

We needed this fuel because we were all active from morning till night. One day we hiked to Anglezarke Reservoir, via Abbey Village, Withnell, Brinscall and White Coppice, crossing the Black Brook en route. A few years later, at University, I read *The Lord of the Rings* and it was this hike that I remembered as I imagined the hobbits' route from The Hill, to Bywater, Buckland, Bree and over the Brandywine River. There were no Nazgûl in pursuit over the moors, purple with heather, though Skipper warned us that if our map-reading skills failed us and we were lost on the moors at night-time, the Bogarts would get us.

It was a hot and sweaty day and flies were bothersome. It was a trek of seven miles there and seven back. We did get lost once or twice - there were few landmarks to guide us - but we soon found our way back to the path again.

The hobbits' first glimpse of Rivendell couldn't have thrilled them as much as our first view of Anglezarke did. As we came to the edge of an escarpment, there suddenly stretched out below us an immense tract of bright blue water in which the reflections of a few high white clouds drifted serenely. We were town boys, after all, and most of us were from families of limited means. One or two of us had been to the Lakes, though nobody had been taken much beyond the tourist venues around Windermere.

This vast panorama was sublime, I felt, though I hardly knew the connotations of the word at the time. The vista of reservoir, chequered fields and dark blue-green forest was dazzling in the late afternoon sun. It tugged at your heart.

I looked at Ben for confirmation that he was feeling the same.

'Fuck me!' he said, aware of my glance but not looking at me. 'Fuck me blind.'

We were exhausted as we trooped back into camp. Supper was Irish stew from tins, with tea and the inevitable hunks of white bread.

We crawled into our tents as soon as we had eaten, though there was still some light in the sky. In our foxhole, we said goodnight to our pet earwig, Clarence, who lived in the junction between the ridge-pole and the upright at the far end. Then I put out the Tilley lamp. An owl shrieked and we tumbled, headlong, into the deepest sleep I can ever remember.

13.   WIDE GAME

WE WERE HAVING A HIGH OLD TIME. A number of highlights are foregrounded in my memory and are running like a trailer from a film. Downstream from our campsite our little brook opened into a pool, deep enough for bathing. Ben had discovered it as he and his patrol were foraging for wood, and they came rushing back with the news. He and Skipper went down to check it out and Skipper gave it the OK.

Grabbing towels, a number of us trotted down to the spot. Four or five of us went in naked; the rest kept their underpants on. Though a scout should be clean in thought, word and deed, after a week in camp, the requirement did not extend to Y-fronts, which, in some cases, were a horrible grey.

Silly daft Jimmy Griffin was one of the skinny-dippers. He ripped off his uniform and went charging through a patch of weeds into the water. Unfortunately the weeds turned out to be stinging nettles and his whoops of excitement turned to screams. When he emerged his body was covered in red lumps from the waist down. Somebody ran for Skipper, who had gone back to the bell-tent, and he came and carried Jimmy to the first-aid tent.

To be honest, there wasn't much room for swimming in the pool once there were a dozen of us in there. The water only came up to my belly button and the bed of the stream was muddy and squelchy and you got bits of weed and twig between your toes. But it was fine for splashing and wrestling. It was a scorching hot day and the little glade where the pool had formed was cool and shady. We played until the mud was all churned up and the water murky and brown. Then we towelled ourselves down, dressed, and went back to camp to find out the fate of poor Jimmy.

The hapless lad was running a temperature and Skip finally decided he ought to be checked out in Casualty. Ken, who had followed the lorry in his mini, drove him off to the Infirmary. He didn't come back to camp - poor beggar - and was poorly for several days.

On another occasion, Skipper and Ken rigged up an aerial cable for us over a deep gully upstream. I suppose nowadays you would call it a zipwire. One end of the cable was fastened to a kind of elevated tripod, built from scaffolding poles, which the scoutmasters erected on one side of the stream. The other end of the cable was attached to a tree on the far bank, which was much lower down. You put your foot in a rope loop hanging from a pulley and held on to a hook with both hands and went whizzing down the cable, screaming and laughing with glee. A pulley at the top of the tripod allowed us to be hauled back to the starting point. We could not get enough of this and went backwards and forwards all afternoon. It was a sad moment when it all had to be dismantled, but the prospect of bangers and beans round the fire was some compensation.

Best of all was the Wide Game which we played on the last night of camp. In the afternoon, Skipper summoned the patrol leaders to the bell-tent, spread out a map of the area on a trestle table, and explained the boundaries which we were honour bound to observe. To the north the boundary was the road by which we'd arrived; to the west, the gate to the farmyard; to the east, a drystone wall which led to the point where the aerial cable had been erected. To the south there was the stream and beyond it, woodland. The frontier in the wood was a wire fence about two hundred yards in.

We drew lots. Ben's Beavers were to be the hunters and the other two patrols were to be the hunted. They would set off from the bell tent at intervals and the Beavers had to stay in the tent so that they couldn't see which direction the other teams had taken. Then they would be released. Their objective was to capture the other patrols by tagging them. Patrols had to stick together and could not split up.

There was a time limit. Each of the three patrol leaders was given a roman candle. If the Beavers captured the other two patrols within the time, Ben could let off his firework. Skipper and Ken, back at camp, would be looking out for the signal. If, on the other hand, a hunted patrol managed to last the time without being caught, their patrol leader could light his firework.

'Make sure you keep them dry,' Skipper said. 'They should really be flares.'

'Aw,' Ben said. 'Why can't we have proper flares?'

'Because,' Skip said.

'Because what?' Ben persisted.

'Because you need a licence to use a flare gun and you're not old enough anyway,' Skip said.

'Aw!' Ben said.

'Nark it!' Skip said, 'and stop bellyaching, Ben Westwell.'

Ben pulled one of his more expressive faces.

Later that afternoon, I got the rest of my patrol making pilchard sandwiches for tea whilst I went off with Dave Forbes, my trusty number 2, to do a recce. I wasn't worried about Hound Patrol. They were bound to cock it up. But I was desperate to defeat Ben's Beavers. During a pretty intensive survey of the territory within the boundaries, we made a most interesting discovery.

Back at our site, I explained my battle plan to the rest of the patrol. The butties were soggy but delicious; the tea was as black as treacle and had its usual flotilla of tiny insects on top but, sweetened with spoonfuls of Carnation condensed milk, nobody cared. And the plan, everybody agreed, was genius.

That evening, as soon as it was dark, we met up in the bell-tent and solemnly synchronised our watches. Hound Patrol set off first and ten minutes later we were released. I had calculated that everyone would head for the woods on the other side of the river and I wanted Ben to think that was our plan too. We sprinted off, leaving a very obvious trail through some long grass, but when we got to the little stream I signalled to the others to stop and listen. There was nothing but the chuckling of the water over the pebbles and the melancholy hooting of owls in the wood. If Ben's patrol were stalking us, they were very good at it.

At this point, the brook was quite shallow and fast-flowing on our side, with a firm rocky bed. We walked downstream in the water for perhaps twenty yards like they do in westerns and crime films. Obviously, Ben didn't have an Indian scout or a team of tracker dogs to sniff us out, but it seemed like a smart thing to do.

We stepped out of the water at different points, and brushed out our tracks on the sandy bank with fallen branches. Though the moon was full, the moonlight was not strong enough to betray any sign that we had passed that way. Any pursuer would have had to use a torch - an obvious giveaway.

We were close now to the drystone wall at the eastern boundary. Ahead of us was a slope covered with scrub. We moved up it on our bellies, using our elbows for propulsion. Whether this was a technique we'd also learnt from films or whether it was advised in *Scouting for Boys* I can't remember, but it felt pretty authentic. We passed our campsite somewhere to our left and came to a yard where there stood a mud-caked tractor, some farm machinery covered with spikes, which had been left to die of rust, or so it seemed, and a derelict barn. Dave and I had already decided during our reconnoitre earlier that it was too obvious as a hiding place.

In the yard there were also three disused chicken coops. Two of them were smashed in and roofless, with chickweed growing up through the shattered floor. The third, however, was intact. When we first found it the floor was deep in snail shells and black and white chicken shit like liquorice allsorts. Dave and I had scraped all this away from the doorway and to the back.

Dave led my little foxes into the coop and I crept in last, pulling the small arched door to behind me. It was very rickety on its one remaining hinge but it would have to do.

We waited a very long time, over an hour, sitting there in silence in the pitch dark.

At one point, as I felt I might be drifting off to sleep, a plaintive voice said:

'I want to wee.'

It was little Jeff Holden, who'd only come up from the cubs two weeks earlier.

The others shushed him viciously.

'You'll have to hold it or do it there' I said, trying to sound kind. 'It won't be long now. Try to think of something else.'

It's not easy trying to sound kind in a whisper.

'All right,' Jeff replied in a tiny voice.

I felt very proud of him and all my gang, to be honest.

After an age we heard the sound of a lorry or a truck on the path from the farm and then the crunch of tyres as the vehicle swung into the yard. Muted laughter and indistinct men's voices reached us in our den and then heavy boots crunched away across the yard and silence fell again.

But not for long.

After a couple of minutes we heard a boy's voice instead. It was Ben and he was very close, just outside the coop.

'I don't get it,' he said. 'What's the sly git up to? We've looked everywhere.'

'What about the barn?' another voice said.

'We've looked,' Ben said. 'It's all smashed open. There's nowhere for six boys to hide.'

'What about this?' Somebody kicked the side of the coop.

I could feel the boys on either side of me tense up.

A couple of fierce kicks and the door fell in, its one remaining hinge giving way at last. Torchlight flickered around the space inside and fell on the great pile of droppings which Dave and I had scraped into a heap opposite the door. We were sitting along the same wall as the doorway, our feet pulled up tight. The torch beam didn't reach us.

'Eeeuw!' a voice said. 'It's full of chicken-shit.'

'Leave it,' Ben said. 'They're not up here. We've only got twelve minutes left. Come on. Back to the wood.'

They ran off chattering. They'd obviously given up on any idea of stealth. It sounded as if there were quite a lot of them and I guessed that they must have captured Hound Patrol earlier in the game.

We breathed again.

With my torch carefully shielded, I counted down the final minutes.

'We've done it, lads!' I yelled, and we piled out of the coop, brushing off straw and droppings.

The moonlight was brighter now and there was a distinct chill. Steam rose from in front of Jeff, who was relieving himself. You wouldn't have expected such a powerful stream from such a little chap.

'Oh God,' he said. 'Oh God, that's good!'

Meanwhile, I steadied the Roman candle in a little pile of stones and lit it. It fizzed - there was a fountain of golden sparks, which grew more intense, and then it shot balls of fire into the sky: crimson, green and white, telling the world that we had won.

Elated, we hurtled back down to camp, stumbling over tussocky grass as we went. Shortly afterwards the others trooped back, dejected just for the moment.

We had won but Ben wasn't having it.

'Where were you?' he asked.

'In the chicken coop,' I said.

'No, you weren't. We looked.'

'Well, you didn't look hard enough, did you?'

'But that's cheating,' Ben said. He appealed to Skipper. 'They cheated, didn't they, Skip?'

'How were they cheating?' Skip said.

'Staying in one place all the time,' Ben said.

'I'd call that enterprise, not cheating,' Skip said.

'And it's only what we did after all,' said Harry, leader of Hound Patrol.

'You lot were pathetic,' Ben laughed.

'Why?' I said. 'What did they do?'

'We climbed a tree,' Harry said, grinning.

'They climbed a ruddy great oak tree on the other side of the brook,' Ben said. 'They climbed really high up an' all and I reckon it would have been fab except...'

'Except what?' I said.

'Except they were whispering and giggling,' said Ben, 'and turning their torches on and off. It were like a bloomin' Christmas tree. We found them in about ten minutes.'

'It were fair enough,' Harry laughed. He was a cheery lad and maybe his sense of fair play persuaded Ben that it would be churlish to continue sulking. That and the fact that Skip said he and Harry could set off their Roman candles now.

Skipper and Ken had hot tomato soup ready for us, and they had built a bonfire which they now lit. We sat around it on logs, cradling tin mugs of soup with Benson's potato crisps crumbled on top. Benson's came with salt in a twist of dark blue paper in the packet, and we sprinkled the salt over the crisps, which went soggy.

As the flames leapt and the heart of the fire began to glow a deep pink colour, Skipper told a yarn, a kind of Red Indian ghost story, and then we had a sing-song. We sang *Riding along on the Crest of a Wave* and *Ging-Gang Goolie*, and *The Quartermaster's Stores*.

My eyes are dim I cannot see
I have not brought my specs with me
I have no-ot brought my-y specs with me...

As we sang the refrain, I saw that Ben was merely mouthing the words as he stared into the depths of the fire, lost in the kind of trance I had seen before.

We had struck camp that afternoon and my patrol and I said goodbye to Clarence the earwig as I persuaded him to crawl on to my finger and let him loose into the grass. That night the whole troop slept in the great bell-tent, lying like the spokes of a wheel, our feet towards the central pole.

It was cosy and safe.

The next morning the lorry came to collect us and after we'd unloaded it back in the den, we separated and trudged home.

'It feels weird, doesn't it?' said Ben as we walked home together. 'Being on our own again.'

'I know what you mean,' I said.

'Good lord,' Mum said when I arrived home. 'Look at the state of you. You're absolutely filthy. Get in the bath this minute.'

I had not been conscious of this until she mentioned it. Soon I lay in the bath, lapped in warmth as steam misted the mirror and I picked a scab on my knee.

Mum was right as usual. As I lay there, dreamy and happy, a grey scum rose to the surface of the bathwater.

14.   BLACK EYE

I SOMETIMES THINK I SHOULD have read the signs. More than once I'd noticed that rapt, transfixed gaze in Ben's eyes as he looked into the heart of the fire.

I saw it - it registered with me as strange - but I didn't think to interpret it. Why would I? Kids of that age are not particularly reflective creatures - I certainly wasn't.

But there were other signs of a darkness in my friend's life to which I should perhaps have paid more attention - though heaven knows there was little I could have done about it.

Once, when we were still at St John's, he came to school with a black eye.

'How did you get that?' I said. 'It's a right shiner.'

'Walked into a door,' Ben said.

'No, you didn't,' I said.

'All right then. If you know better you can suit yersen.'

'You want to put a raw steak on that. That's what they do in *The Beano*.'

'Where am I going to get a steak from? We're lucky to get luncheon meat in our house.'

'You'd look a right wazzock with luncheon meat on your face. It has to be steak. You need to get a dog to nick one from the butcher's. That's what they'd do in *The Beano*.'

'You read too much, you do, Stewpot. Now drop it.'

'Come on,' I persisted. 'You can tell me. I'm your best mate.'

'If you must know, it were me dad.'

'Never,' I said.

It didn't fit. I hadn't seen Mr Westwell very often, not since I was very small when we did sleep overs. I thought he was a nice, kind man.

Even though I still dropped off at Ben's house after school most days, I rarely saw his dad because he didn't get home till long after I had to go off for my tea. That he'd be violent with his own kid was hard to believe. On the other hand, I didn't think Ben would lie to me.

'How did it happen?' I said.

'Right, well, you know Sandra, right? Well, she were getting on my wick as usual. I warned her but she wouldn't stop so I twatted her one. It weren't that hard but she's as soft as butter and she started skriking and she said she'd tell Mum.'

'Did she?'

'Too right she did. Mum said I wasn't too old for a right belting and I told her she'd have to catch me first. "Wait till your dad gets home," she said, like she always does.'

'Normally she forgets but this time she didn't. Mum grassed me up with Sandra chiming in and Dad grabbed hold of me and dragged me upstairs and slapped me about quite a bit. I could smell the beer on him. He'd have stopped off at the Craven Heifer for a couple of jars on the way home from work, like he usually did.

'Sandra's Daddy's darling, you see. Can't do no wrong, she can't. You should have seen her horrible smarmy little face when I finally came downstairs looking like a bloody panda. Mum burst into tears but she didn't say owt.'

This story unsettled me. I was sorry for my mate, obviously, but I didn't hold with hitting girls, even if they were annoying, which they usually were. I couldn't square my image of his dad with the drunken brute who'd beaten him up. And why didn't his mum protect him? My mum would have.

'Does it hurt?' I said.

'Only when I fart,' he said, and ran off laughing.

I knew that the teachers were concerned when Miss Marsden asked Ben to stay behind after a recorder lesson. It was our first one and the others had got as far as producing a simple scale. I'd managed nothing apart from high-pitched shrieks until Miss Marsden pointed out that I should have my thumb over the hole underneath. I complained bitterly that I didn't even know that there was a hole underneath. The others had hysterics at my expense. Ben laughed the loudest and played the opening of *Frère Jacques* to make me look even more thick. He'd been practising in secret, the smartypants.

Anyway, his face fell when he was asked to stay behind.

We trooped out and I stood on tiptoe to peer through the glass panel in the door at Ben, standing with his hands behind his back in front of the teacher's desk. She saw me and waved me away.

He came out a few minutes later grinning all over his face.

'What was all that about?' I said.

'She said that I am probably the best recorder player that she's ever heard and that she's going to get me a concert in King George's Hall on Saturday.'

He did his cherubic innocence face.

'Did she 'eck as like,' I said. 'Go on, what were it really about?'

'My black eye.'

'And?'

'I said I'd walked into a door.'

'And did she believe you?'

'Don't know. Not bothered. Who cares?' he said, as he breezed off down the corridor.

I thought no more about it until an occasion more than a year later when I accidentally came across further evidence of Ben's father's potential for violence.

In 1961, both Ben and I won scholarships to the grammar school. It was a time of great upheaval and I'll have more to say about school later. But there was another change which I now think affected our friendship, though nothing was ever said at the time. If I'm right, the effect was very gradual.

Just before I changed schools, my family moved house. My dad was some sort of civil servant and he had been doing well. I've always been pretty incurious about his employment. I've no idea which department he was in, for instance, and to be honest I might even have been a little bit snobbish about it because I thought it sounded very boring. Anyway, he'd been promoted and his new rank meant a considerable increase in salary.

We didn't move far, just round the corner to Whalley Range. There was quite a big difference from the two-up-two-down at Brookhouse Lane. Our new house was on a row built on a grassed-over embankment, and stone steps led up to the front door. At the back of the house was a little garden which was also on a slope. Dad said he was going to grow our own vegetables and maybe chrysanthemums.

There was lots more space. There was a hallway instead of a door opening on to the street; there was a separate dining room with a big fireplace and a high ceiling; a spacious kitchen - but best of all, there was a bathroom. No more shivering in an outdoor lav. No more chamber pots under the bed. I felt we'd gone up in the world. And I was chuffed.

It never occurred to me that Ben might feel left behind in some way. Our friendship didn't seem to be materially affected. Even when we moved to QEGS, I always walked home with him, stopping off at his house for an hour or so while he laid the fire, and we would sometimes do a bit of homework together.

One autumn afternoon we'd done some Latin exercises. Latin was still new and quite exciting, but it was hard and so it was helpful for us to put our heads together to work out that the farmer loved his pigs and that the army had marched through the wood and crossed the river. Ben said that we had to be quiet because his mum hadn't gone to work and was poorly upstairs. Sandra had been sent to an auntie's for the day.

It wasn't until I got home and was emptying my satchel that I realised I had left my Latin exercise book at Ben's. We had done the exercises in rough and I needed to copy them up before the next day because Mr Oliphant, the Latin master, was pretty scary. There was nothing for it. I would have to go back and get it.

Nobody locked their front doors back then. I just walked in, through the dark, unused front room and into the brightly lit living room-cum-kitchen.

'I forgot my Latin book,' I said.

Mrs Westwell, who had her back to me and was frying something on the stove, turned to look at me.

What I saw was very shocking. Her left eye was so badly bruised it was a mere slit in a purple-yellow swelling; the whole of that side of her face was puffed up; there was dried blood around her left nostril and her nose looked crooked; there were blackened cuts on her lower lip, which was also swollen.

She turned away in embarrassment as soon as she saw me.

Ben whipped the yellow exercise book from the table and thrust it into my hands.

'I think you should just go,' he said. 'Come on.'

And he practically manhandled me back through the front room and into the street.

'What's up with your mum?' I said. 'She looks terrible.'

'Not now, Stewpot,' he said. 'I'll see you tomorrow.'

And he shut the door in my face, leaving me standing alone in the empty street.

A scruffy mongrel appeared from nowhere and had a sniff at the lamppost by which I was standing, thought better of it, looked at me slyly and slunk down the street to the next one. It had begun to rain, a thin fine rain.

It was not hard to work out what had happened to Ben's mum.

I stood there in the mizzle, appalled.

15.   DIVIDED LOYALTIES

WE WALKED TO SCHOOL THE FOLLOWING DAY in silence. I met Ben as usual at the top of Brookhouse Lane and we walked all the way along Randal Street to Limbrick and through the ginnel to Preston New Road. He didn't say a word and I couldn't think of any way to start a conversation. I tried to imagine what the atmosphere in his house must have been like the previous evening before he pushed me out into the street, but I failed.

I looked at him from time to time but his face was set.

By the time we were walking up through the park, I couldn't stand it any longer. I had to speak, if only to show him somehow that I was loyal. It was pretty gormless, I suppose, but all I could think of to say was: 'Was he drunk?'

Ben just nodded. I knew better than to press him. At last we parted to go to our separate form rooms.

Ben and I had been close for as long as I could remember. We had been together in the infants and the juniors. I could even remember as far back as reception class: A for Apple, B for Ball, C for Cat. We already knew the alphabet but some of the others needed to catch up. In the afternoons we were supposed to have a little sleep. There were canvas beds with metal frames. We could rarely manage to drift off, and I remember us being told off for peeking at each other through our fingers and giggling. Ben's coat peg was a squirrel and mine was a frog. The squirrel was blue for some reason.

When we arrived at QEGS we were put into different forms: I went into 2A and Ben into 2B (- the first forms were in the prep school). I suppose the setting was based on 11+ results but I was mystified by this. I had always thought of Ben as being brighter than me. He seemed, on the surface at least, to take it stoically, but it gradually became clear that it sapped his motivation. He was still really competitive in the scouts, and even in the choir, but at school, it was as if he couldn't be bothered.

Though we still did our homework together, quite often mine was more advanced than his, and, to tell the truth, I usually ended up doing his exercises for him. It was no skin off my nose and he was content to let it happen. In class, however, he slipped further and further behind. He did no revision for the end of year exams and performed disastrously. After the summer, I stayed in the A stream and Ben was moved down to 3C. He met the demotion with a shrug.

'So what?' he said. 'It doesn't matter.'

It was around this time that the unreasonableness of adults began to get on my wick. I had always tried to be obliging and respectful and as a result I felt my teachers liked me and went out of their way to encourage me. All the same, I think they had as little understanding of our world as we had of what went on behind the staff room doors.

There was one occasion in particular when I really thought I had been let down by the grown-ups because they put me in an impossible position.

You don't see it now but back then there were lots of parades and processions. When I was quite small, I remember hearing the sound of a band, and Mum and I went out to see what was going on. It was a procession from St Alban's, the Catholic Church at the far end of Brookhouse Lane. There was a great banner with the Virgin Mary on it. Two men carried the poles at either side, and there were guy ropes held by boys, which helped keep it upright in the wind. There were girls in white dresses and boys in white shirts with little bow ties. First communion, Mum said.

There were also quite a number of smiling Polish people in national dress, the boys and men with beautifully embroidered waistcoats, the women and girls with embroidered bodices, full, brightly-coloured skirts and white aprons trimmed with lace.

At St John's each year there would be a procession for the crowning of the Rose Queen. This was a pretty girl from the top class. She wore a white dress, a crown and a red cloak. The previous year's queen would also be there, wearing a blue cloak. They would ride in triumph on thrones on a decorated float, a lorry in festive disguise.

Normally, Ben and I thought ourselves above all this girly stuff and, in any case, as choristers, we would be right at the front of the procession behind the silver cross. One year, however, his sister Sandra was chosen as the May Queen. In her coronation dress and cloak, I thought she looked very beautiful and I made the mistake of mentioning this to Ben.

'Are you off your rocker?' he said. 'She's about as beautiful as a rhinoceros's arse and a bloody sight less intelligent. I've got all the looks in our family - and the brains.'

Even QEGS had a procession once a year for the annual carol service in the Cathedral. We walked into town in form groups, juniors at the front, the masters wearing academic gowns and hoods over their overcoats walking alongside to maintain good discipline. All those ranks of blue uniforms must have been quite a sight. A policeman held up the traffic as we passed through Sudell Cross.

One year there was a terrible fuss. Apparently, a sizeable troop of sixth formers, who had been marching unsupervised at the back of the procession, executed a smart right turn after we passed the Town Hall, and disappeared into Marks and Spencers in order to avoid the service and the sermon.

But I'm digressing. The clash of interests I mentioned involved the scouts and the choir. Once a month there was a church parade at Holy Trinity, which was a bit of a problem because, if Ben and I attended, Mr Butterfield stood to lose two of his choristers. Whatever we chose to do, we would be made to feel guilty. Usually, we chose the choir, perhaps with some vague feeling that we could cope with Skip being miffed with us, but not God.

The previous year, the sense of divided loyalties became particularly intense. Church Parade would be held on April 22nd and, as St George's Day was on the Monday immediately following, there would be added pomp and circumstance. We would parade the flags through the streets ahead of a brass band: the flag of

St George alongside the union flag, the green scout flag, the blue guide flag, the yellow wolf cub flag, and the little leather pennant of the brownies. There would be the usual splendid banners, of the church and the Mothers' Union, following behind. It would be very grand. Skipper said he wanted me to be the bearer of the scout flag, which I considered a very great honour.

Unfortunately, in 1962, April 22nd was Easter Day.

'What can you have been thinking of, boys?' Mr Butterfield said, when Ben and I asked permission to attend church parade. 'The Easter Sung Eucharist is the most important service of the year. Out of the question. You need to be here.'

And much as I loved a parade, we could see his point. There would be no shortage of ritual at St John's, I supposed. On Good Friday we would attend a lugubrious service, wearing cassocks only, no sur-plices. The altar would be stripped to the bare wood and all decoration removed from the church. Then on the Saturday we would go to the fair in the market place while the ladies filled the church with flowers and the altar front was changed to white. And on the Sunday there would be amazing music in the trans-figured church which we'd been rehearsing for weeks.

Skipper was not best pleased with us, and Ben and I grumbled to each other that it was unfair.

This year, however, Easter fell earlier in the month and was done and dusted by the time of the St George's parade at Holy Trinity. This time Skipper had an irresistible bribe for me. I was to carry the union flag and this time Mr Butterfield would not prevail.

I took it home with me in its leather case and polished the brass spear head at the top until it dazzled. The flag itself was really impressive with a border of gold braid, and there were two cords of red, white and blue with tassels.

I also felt that I needed to practise a particular manoeuvre. On the day, we would march around the local streets to the beat of the big bass drum (*Holy Trinity 3rd Blackburn* in big letters at the circumference) and the more or less tuneful blare of bugles. ('Just mime,' Skip had said to Jimmy Griffin in rehearsal because he could only produce horrible shrieking noises.) Then the procession would file into the church. The flag bearers would take up positions in the chancel and the vicar would collect the flags one by one, and they would be placed around the sanctuary. Towards the end of the service they would be rededicated and returned to their bearers.

It was at this point that my big moment would come. I would move to the centre of the chancel and advance to the sanctuary steps. Then, as everyone belted out the national anthem, I would take the pole out of the holster, put it under my right arm, and slowly and steadily lower it until the tip touched the carpet and the flag itself was draped theatrically across the steps.

This is why I needed to practise. The flag was surprisingly heavy when held like this and the whole movement had to be smooth. What if I dropped the bloody thing? What if I couldn't get it back in the holster again? It would all be very public. Though I was thirteen and a half, I had some vague feeling that Her Majesty would get to hear that I'd made a gormless mess of the ceremony. And, of course, God sees everything. A terrible responsibility had fallen upon me.

But there was an even more profound reason why it had to be exactly right. The choir of Holy Trinity, unlike St John's choir, had girls in it. This seemed to me to be very strange and, somehow, even *wrong*.

However, I was prepared to overlook this travesty because I had fallen in love with one of them. Her name was Jean Forbes and she was the older sister of my Patrol Second, Dave. We had first met at Dave's house on Cleaver Street when I called for him on the way to scouts. I say 'met' but the truth is, she barely acknowledged me. She was two years older and that was enough. It was hopeless.

I couldn't tell Dave that I was passionately in love with his sister. I certainly couldn't tell Ben, not after the response I got when I told him I thought his sister was growing up to look very pretty.

There was an outfitter's called Johnny Forbes in Blackburn at the time. It's where you got school uniforms, and my cub and scout uniforms had come from there too. I think their shop was on Northgate - maybe it still is. They were well known and advertised widely. They were nothing to do with Jean and Dave but I could not see an advertisement for 'Forbes' in the *Lancashire Evening Telegraph* - or even the school magazine - without thinking of Jean and melting into secret grief in the face of my unattainable love.

Before the event I had a dream. A drum roll announced the national anthem. I took the flag out of the holster. I was vividly aware of Jean standing in the front stalls of *decani*, behind me and to my right. I began to dip the flag when suddenly I was shot in the left shoulder, no doubt by a Russian spy. Though the pain was traumatic, I managed to complete the homage ceremony to perfection. Only when I had returned the flag to the upright did I collapse in agony, and Ben stepped forward to take the flag from me and prevent it from falling dishonourably to the ground. When I recovered, Jean declared herself won over by my courage, so we married and were happy ever after.

At the time I would have died rather than have anyone know about this dream. I was mortified by the childish silliness of it.

In the event, I performed my duty impeccably. Ben wasn't even there. He had decided to attend the service at St John's.

What - if anything - Jean thought, I have no idea.

16.   SCHOOL

I CAN'T REMEMBER NOW how long my grand passion for Jean Forbes lasted. Not long, I think. It burned with ravenous intensity for a few weeks but, because it hadn't a hope in hell of being requited, it devoured its own fuel and starved itself of oxygen. One morning, walking to school up through the park, I realised that love had released me from the stake. I felt liberated.

I sometimes walked to school on my own now. There was a gradual loosening of the bonds between me and Ben once we went up to the grammar school. He was often late. I would wait for him at the top of Brookhouse Lane until waiting any longer would make me late too. He said he found it hard to get out of bed in the morning and just ignored his mother when she called him. Whether she was powerless to do anything about it, once her husband had gone to work, or whether she was past caring, given the pasting both of them had suffered at his hands, I don't know. His sister would probably have grassed him up but she went to school by bus and left pretty early.

I would never have got away with it. On the couple of occasions when I'd tried it, Mum had come upstairs, yanked the bedclothes off me and hurled them down the stairs.

On the mornings when Ben chose to lie in, I would meet Tom coming up Brookhouse Lane and would walk on to school without him.

'Where were you this morning?' he would say occasionally. 'I waited for you.'

'We'd already gone,' I would say. 'I never know whether you're coming or whether you're still in bed.'

'Fair enough,' he'd say. 'Some mornings I just need more beauty sleep, you know.'

'It's not working.'

'What isn't?'

'Beauty sleep. You look like Plug from *The Beano*.'

'Get stuffed, you. I'm gorgeous and you know it.'

Even though he was constantly bollocked for being late and earned no end of detentions it made no difference. When his form master said that if Ben were late again he'd be writing home, I thought that must be the end of it, but no. Ben was late the very next day. Mr Charnley told him at afternoon registration that a letter had gone to his father. When he told me about it, I was afraid that Ben would get a terrible belting.

Believe it or not, he was late the next morning too. When he arrived, at morning break as usual, he gleefully showed us Charnley's letter which he'd intercepted.

'I just stayed in bed till Mum went to work, got up, made some toast and waited for the postman,' he said, and waltzed off, singing: *Please, Mr Postman, look and see. Is there a letter in your bag for me?*

He was always getting into scrapes.

Science lessons were seated and Ben was good enough at Chemistry for us to be in the same set. There was no seating plan and we used to sit together He often got me into trouble, usually for chatting, but sometimes worse. I would have preferred not to get on the wrong side of Mr Maddox, if possible. His punishments were notorious. It was to be a couple of decades before corporal punishment was banned in British school, but it was relatively rare at QEGS. However, the Madman, as we called him, had a nasty way of creeping up behind you in the lab and cracking you one on the back of the head if you were nattering. He would happily clobber both of you, one with each hand.

But this was small beer. He was really the past master of more extended forms of torture. A geologist by training, he had a collection of rocks. Villains would have to stand at the front, holding out a sizeable lump of rock at arm's length until agony was inscribed on their faces. This was 'Baby Rock'. Repeat villains were made to hold out an even bigger boulder, known as 'Daddy Rock'. There was no appeal to 'yooman rights' back then. Ben and Daddy Rock were well-acquainted.

These torments were as nothing compared to the 'Cricket Square Torture' and 'Death by Graph Paper'. The Madman was a cricket fanatic and a member of the East Lancs Cricket Club who had grounds next door to the school. On (for him) festive occasions, he would take a delegation of offenders round there and have them trimming the edges of the cricket square armed only with nail scissors.

'Death by Graph Paper' was by far the worst of his medieval tortures. If you really got his goat, he would simply hand you a sheet of graph paper. We all knew what it meant. Before the next Chemistry lesson, you had to pierce every minute square on the sheet with the point of a compass. This had to be done with extreme care. Obviously, the paper became very fragile and you couldn't afford to tear it or you'd have to start again. If you got it to the Madman intact, he would put it on the overhead projector. 'He's missed one!' the class would shout, more often than not. The Madman would simply hand out another sheet of graph paper, wordlessly, but with a serene and satanic smile.

Ben got me into trouble more than once in Chemistry and he certainly didn't help me academically when we worked in pairs. I remember some experiment in which we were supposed to heat some magnesium in a crucible quite fiercely, measuring it before and after, in order to calculate the mass of the gas that had been acquired in the oxidisation. Of course, the crucible should have been heavier but in our case the damn thing was much lighter.

I think this was because Ben kept lifting the crucible lid with the small tongs that had been supplied in order for us to see what was happening. Little sparks and powdery ash must have escaped each time. When I protested, he told me not to be an old woman and persuaded Tom Catlow and his partner further up the bench to let us copy their results in return for the promise of a couple of bags of crisps the following day. Ben adjusted the figures in the table we copied, just enough to be credible and yet unsuspicious. That time, wc got away with it.

I'd noticed earlier that, when the Madman was issuing the magnesium ribbon, he'd put down the roll on the bench whilst he was answering some nerdy question from Tom, who was an enthusiastic Chemistry boffin. Whilst he was showing him the relevant detail in the textbook, Ben had managed to tear off a sizeable strip of the ribbon and hide it in his pocket. I knew what he was going to do and was filled with foreboding.

Once an experiment had been set up Maddox had a habit of disappearing into the prep room to talk about cricket with the lab assistant, whom we called Igor. On more than one of these occasions, Ben had entertained the class by throwing purloined iron filings into the flame of a Bunsen burner. The filings would melt and burst, sparkling and crackling like fireworks. On each occasion, he'd got away without being caught. Today, he was not so lucky.

The Madman had disappeared as usual. I was copying up the massaged results into my exercise book when Ben gave me a nudge and produced the ribbon from his pocket. He gave me a depraved kind of a wink. Using the tongs for the crucible lid he introduced the ribbon into the Bunsen flame. There was a flare of dazzling white light just as Maddox re-emerged from the prep room.

Panicking, Ben threw the still burning ribbon into the waste basket behind us, which was full of paper and promptly burst into flames.

Maddox grabbed a fire extinguisher and put out the flames, pretty deftly, I have to say. Then he beckoned to both of us to come to the master's demonstration bench.

I put my fingers to my chest and raised my eyebrows in a 'What? Me?' gesture and Maddox nodded gravely.

It was useless to protest that I was one hundred per cent innocent. Maddox had made his mind up. Sheepishly, we went up to the front.

Not looking at us, but gazing impassively at the rest of the class, he handed each of us a sheet of graph paper.

We turned to go back to our places.

'No, no, no,' he said, and handed us another sheet each.

Back on our stools, I whispered to Ben, 'I'm going to beat the shit out of you when we get outside.'

'You can try,' he said, his eyes dancing with laughter.

17. A SLIPPERY SLOPE

I CAN'T REMEMBER if there was a fight. I doubt it. We bantered and bickered all the time and there had been clumsy wrestling play fights when we were younger but I don't remember a proper scrap - not one where blows were landed. He was still my best mate and no doubt we took the rap together.

But the drifting apart continued and Ben was going cheerfully off thc rails. This was not something I remember thinking about consciously. Just as our childhood intimacy was an unreflective thing, so our estrangement was imperceptible until it was complete.

'Like two peas in a pod,' Mrs Haydock had said in the Co-op.

That was hardly true any more. Ben wore his bright blond hair in a Beatles' mop, while mine had darkened several shades and I wore it rather shorter in conformity with school rules. I was taller than him by now, by an inch or so, I reckon.

His voice broke before mine and he decided to leave the choir at St John's. Mr Butterfield had wanted him to join the men in due course but Ben said it was no good: one minute he would be talking in a bass voice and then there would be a squeak or a croak. Ben said he'd forgotten how to sing and Mr B said his voice would soon settle. Ben shook his head glumly and said it was no good. In private he told me that he'd enjoyed being out of the ordinary as a treble but saw no future in being a mediocre bass.

He left the scouts soon after that.

'Why?' I asked him.

'It's for kids,' he said.

'You don't believe that,' I said.

'Yeah, I do,' he said. 'All that tying knots and sa-luting flags and playing at soldiers. And all that 'lads together' crap. It's unnatural.'

'Don't give me that. You love it,' I said. 'You like the competition. You thrive on it. You crave it.'

'Not with you around, I don't.'

'Oh, for God's sake, you're not talking about the chicken shed business, are you?'

'If the woggle fits,' he said.

I let it drop, though I was surprised the Wide Game business still rankled with him. I didn't have him down as a bearer of grudges.

But choir was no fun without him. I missed hide and seek among the gravestones; I missed him pulling faces at me from the stall opposite; most of all I missed our friendly rivalry. Some of the music was becoming too familiar somehow, and the sermons seemed to grow longer. I stopped turning up for choir practice and then to services. There was nothing much poor Mr Butterfield could do about it.

When the Head of Music at school had learned that I was in St John's choir, he kept putting pressure on me to join the Choral Society, but I wasn't having it. I wanted to put the whole singing thing behind me.

Before long, I dropped the scouts too. Again, it wasn't anything like as much fun without Ben. I had no excuses to offer and I didn't want to lie, so I just stopped going. I knew Skipper would be disappointed as he gradually realised I wasn't coming back, and I felt guilty about it. I still do, all these years later. It was an act of cowardice.

A couple of months after I'd made my decision, I saw him outside Mercer's on Northgate and gave him the scouts' three-fingered salute. It was almost involuntary, a reflex action. He didn't return the salute. He just nodded gravely in acknowledgement but did not stop to talk. I knew immediately that I'd hurt him and felt like a worm.

At school, Ben was getting into trouble. He had more or less given up on academic work and his exam results at the end of the second year were so dismal that he was moved down to the D stream. We no longer did our homework together because it was usually at a different level, and in fact I ceased walking home with him and stopping off at Brookhouse Lane.

If he wasn't playing truant he was playing football and he stayed behind after school most days to practise. Apparently, he was a gifted centre forward. I knew this because he'd told me so himself. It also seemed to be the consensus. He was playing in the first XI when he was still much younger than the rest of the team, and there were even rumours that his precocious skills were so necessary to the school's soccer prowess that some of his more rebellious behaviour was overlooked.

I don't know if this was true or not but he was hardly ever out of trouble, that's for sure. He was caught smoking time and time again and it was pretty miraculous that he got away with it, or, at worst, earned a detention.

It was rumoured that Mr Devereux, the Second Master, used to scan the part of Corporation Park opposite the school with binoculars from the staffroom, looking for tell-tale streams of smoke rising from the rhododendron bushes. Then a battalion of prefects would be sent in to flush out the wrong-doers.

The prefects of the time had taken to carrying rolled up umbrellas. We younger boys, in other ranks, thought this affectation was rather poncey. It was amusing all the same to watch the 'precs' poking bushes in the park in the hope of puncturing a junior up to no good.

When he was in the fourth form, Ben got himself into much more serious trouble. At the time there was a sweet shop at the bottom of Duke's Brow, which did a roaring trade at lunch times and after school. I think Ben bought his fags there and they turned a blind eye because custom from the boys was so good.

One lunch time, he asked for ten N⁰· 6 and when the shopkeeper turned to get the cigarettes from the shelves behind him, Ben swept up a handful of penny chews from the tray on the counter and stuffed them in his trouser pocket. When the shopkeeper said he was out of N⁰· 6 and would have to get more from the stockroom, Ben couldn't believe his luck, and while the man was gone he grabbed several Mars Bars and Milky Ways. Unluckily for him, the shopkeeper caught him in the act.

Ben did a runner but it was no good. That afternoon, as boys were milling about to go to art or music or science or whatever, a police car was noticed on West Park Road outside Reception, and later two cops, the Headmaster and the shopkeeper were seen visiting certain classes in earnest conversation. Ben was identified pretty quickly of course. His school uniform and his thick blond hair were a dead giveaway.

He was let off with a caution though he came very close to being expelled. I can just imagine him pulling his best contrite face, shedding fake tears, pleading that he didn't know what came over him and promising on his mother's life that he would never do any such thing ever again.

'All that for - what? - five bob's worth of toffees?' Ben said to me later. 'What a performance. I thought they were going to bang me up in Strangeways. And, you know what? I didn't even get my fags.'

'Are they going to expel you?' I said.

'Nah. Just two Saturday detentions and I'm banned from the shop for life,' he said with a shrug. 'They were thinking of dropping me from the football team because they know that that would piss me off - but they need me.'

I had mixed feelings about this episode. A slightly puritanical streak that had perhaps always been there nagged at me that I should distance myself from this common thief - but another part of me secretly admired his recklessness and the blasé way he was taking his punishment.

I couldn't share Ben's enthusiasm for football, either as a player or as a spectator. On games afternoons, I preferred to go swimming at Freckleton Street Baths. Ben was an avid Rovers fan and would watch them play at home whenever he could wheedle money out of his mother, which wasn't often. My dad had taken me to Ewood Park once or twice when I was very small. I remember being passed over the heads of the grown-ups and allowed to sit at the very edge of the pitch with the other small boys. I remember a meat pie and hot Bovril at the interval and a pipe band marching around the pitch but I don't remember a blind thing about the games, except that I was bored out of my wits.

Ben had new friends who shared his football mania and I took to hanging out more and more with Tom Catlow, climber of chimneys and unearther of skeletons. He still lived on Brookhouse Lane and sometimes we would stop off at his place, do some homework and then perhaps take his dog, Mick, for a walk. He was crazy about that dog. Sometimes Mrs Catlow would ask me if I wanted to stay for tea. On other days we would walk on to Whalley Range and Tom would stay at ours for tea.

Once we'd moved to Whalley Range, Ben hardly ever came round. I asked him why once.

'Too posh for the likes of me,' he said with a big grin, 'especially now you have an electric telephone.'

Then he would adopt a BBC presenter's clipped tones.

'*Helleeow*, the Cooper residence here. No, I'm afraid Master Stuart cannot come to the telephone. He is not permitted to converse with scruffs like you. He is an inter-lectural, you see. He is engaged in academic pursuits with his friend, Thomas. It is a much more appropriate friendship. Please don't call again.'

This was cruel and I felt I didn't deserve it. I had never expressed any kind of snobbery towards Ben, or anybody for that matter. At least I didn't think I had. When we moved house, it's true that I felt we'd gone up in the world and I was glad about it. But I was also aware that there were boys at school who lived in bloody mansions by comparison. Again, I was glad that Tom and I were in the A stream and a bit saddened by Ben's demotion to 4D, but I'm sure we never looked down on him as a result or thought of ourselves as superior beings.

I didn't know how to respond. Was this meant to wound? Or was it just banter? Could it be that he was actually jealous of Tom? That didn't seem to be very much in character but you never knew. Ben was not much given to showing his feelings and was impatient with expressions of emotion in others. I knew enough not to show that I was hurt. He would see it as a sign of weakness.

'Well,' I said, 'you're welcome to come round any time if you change your mind.'

'Yeah right,' he said, 'but I've still got my chores to do - and there's always football.'

I thought there was a flicker of repentance in the way he said this.

But maybe not.

18. SPITFIRES, FRIGATES AND A DESTROYER

THE PHONE WAS AN ESSENTIAL ELEMENT in the homework syndicate. Tom and I would do our homework at the dining room table and then ring around our classmates to check and advise. Tom was the class whiz kid in Biology, Maths and Chemistry. My strong points were English and French, at which Tom was mediocre at best. I couldn't really help him with English composition though I was some use with summary and grammar exercises. In French, accents were worth half a mark each, and I would suggest that a translation exercise from English to French, for instance, ought to have, say, 23 acute accents, 14 graves, 2 circumflexes and 2 feminine plural agreements. So it wasn't really cheating. It was symbiotic, as Tom put it.

After tea, we would ring around to other classmates to exchange information with the class boffin in Latin, the Physics swot and so on. Among us all, we had experts in every field. What the masters would have thought of this initiative, I don't know. I suspect they would have taken a very dim view. We thought it resourceful and enterprising. We were learning from one another, after all: an approach which stood me in good stead when I went on to university in later years.

We had grown out of the street games we used to play around Brookhouse. We would go swimming at Belper Street baths and in summer we would play tennis in Corporation Park. We went everywhere on our bikes. I had an ice-blue Raleigh which I adored. Dad had bought it second-hand for £4.10s back when we were less well off. I knew that this was a tidy part of his weekly wage and I was very grateful.

On one occasion we cycled to Bolton Abbey in Yorkshire. I remember freewheeling down a really steep hill, sunlight flickering through leaves in our eyes, feet off the pedals and legs akimbo. At the bottom there was a sign with a big white rose which said: *Welcome to Yorkshire.* A hundred yards further on, and round a bend, another sign with a red rose said: *Welcome to Lancashire.* Not much further on and halfway up a hill was another white rose sign. Obviously, the road meandered backwards and forwards over the boundary between the two counties.

The journey there and back again was over seventy miles and Tom's mum couldn't believe we'd done it in a day, even though we'd set off very early in the morning. Only when I produced a postcard which I'd bought in the village post office did she admit to being very impressed.

'Next time, take the dog with you,' she said. 'He's been following me round like a lost soul all day.'

'Don't be daft, Mum,' Tom said. 'He can't ride a bike.'

'You cheeky beggar,' Mrs Catlow said. 'I expect you want your tea?'

'Yeah,' Tom said. 'And then I'm going straight to bed. I'm shagged out.'

'What about you, Stuart? Do you want to stay for your tea?' Mrs Catlow said. 'And you watch your language, Tom. You're not too big for me to put you over my knee.'

'I think you'll find I am,' Tom said.

'I think I'll get home, Mrs Catlow,' I said. 'I'm worn out as well. Thanks all the same.'

'See,' Mrs Catlow said to Tom. 'Why can't you be polite like Stuart?'

'I *am* polite,' Tom said, '- to Stuart's mum. Aren't I, Stewpot?'

'I'm not getting involved,' I said.

The other thing that Tom and I were into was model-making. There was a shop next door but one to the Whalley Range pub that specialised in Airfix kits. We would stop there on our way back from school and plan which model we would buy next time we had enough pocket money. We had become quite adept at the business of assembling the models after a couple of false starts which ended up in the bin. This was the result of a lack of patience or attempts to finesse the instructions. I think Tom was probably a bit better at building the models, while I was marginally better at painting them.

Our collection was kept in my bedroom because I had more room than Tom had. There was a tank on my bedside table. The dressing table was covered with a blue cloth on which frigates and destroyers sailed. And Dad had hung our Spitfires, Vulcans and Lancaster bombers from the ceiling with fine cord. This hobby would keep us serenely content. We would spend an hour or so on our models and then go downstairs to watch *Wagon Train* or *The Twilight Zone.* Mum would provide us with mugs of tea, tasty Lancashire cheese and TUC biscuits, which we would guzzle until it was time for Tom to go home.

Talking of mothers, Tom and I had just finished work on a beautiful de Havilland Mosquito one evening, about a week after our trip to Bolton Abbey. He had left early to revise for a Latin test the following day. He had barely gone when the door bell rang. It was unusual for us to have visitors in the evenings, unlike in Brookhouse Lane where callers would walk in without knocking, crying 'Yoo-hoo! It's only me!' I was curious and went with Mum to answer the bell. So it was that Ben burst brutally back into my life.

He stood there on the doorstep, scowling and holding a suitcase in one hand. In the other he held a lady's umbrella with pink and yellow roses on it to cover his mother, who looked horribly pale and tragic. A thin Blackburn rain was falling, the kind that seems nothing much but which can drench you to the very bones in no time.

'Teresa, whatever is the matter?' Mum said. 'Come in for goodness' sake. Come in out of the rain. I'll put the kettle on. Stuart, take Ben up to your room while me and your Auntie Teresa have a little chat.'

Though Ben's dad and mine had been mates in the past, in the days of the babysitting arrangements, they had drifted apart when we moved. Our mums, however, had remained good friends. Mrs Westwell wasn't my real auntie, of course, but back then friends of your parents became honorary aunties and uncles.

Auntie Teresa had been my favourite when Ben and I were little and had what would now be called sleep overs. I thought she was very beautiful and fun-loving. I have a photograph of her, taken by my dad, I think, sitting on Ben's tricycle with her knees sticking out, laughing her head off. Poverty and work and bullying had ravaged her good looks and she seemed like a shrunken version of herself as Mum took the suitcase from Ben and ushered her into the kitchen.

Once in my bedroom, Ben threw himself down on my bed with his arms behind his head. I sat cross-legged at the foot.

'Well, come on then,' I said. 'What happened?'

'So this is what you and your pal Tomcat get up to, is it?' Ben said, ignoring me.

'What?'

'Your plastic air force?' he said, looking at the planes hanging from the ceiling.

'Oh that, yeah. And the tanks and battleships,' I said, waving vaguely towards the dressing table.

'I thought making model aeroplanes was what old men did when they retired.'

'Very funny, Ben,' I said. 'Look, what happened? Was it your dad again?'

'Actually, they're pretty smart,' Ben said. 'Yeah. Dad again.'

'What did he do this time? Did he attack you?'

'And Mum.'

He sat up and looked me in the eye.

'It was probably all my fault in the first place,' he said. 'I was the one as started it.'

'How come?'

'Well, he was home early. He said the shop steward had called them out on strike, summat to do with a time and motion study. Anyway, he were sat there, by the fire, reading *The Evening Telegraph*, probably waiting for the pub to open. I were sat on the rug at his feet, playing with my best Zippo lighter and - well, I don't know what came over me - I couldn't resist it - I set fire to the bottom of his paper. It went up like I don't know what!'

'Bloody hell!'

'It were right comical. He stood up, trying to beat the flames out with his hands and get the thing into the fireplace. There were bits of burning paper flying everywhere. And he were swearing summat shocking. Anyway, me mum flies in from the kitchen and says: "What on earth is going on?"

'He says: "Your bloody son has only gone and set fire to my bloody paper" (only, he didn't say "bloody"). "He's your son as well," says me mum, and she burst out laughing at him flailing around with his burning paper. And that set me off as well. We were hysterical.

'Well, that were it. He got the flaming mess into the fireplace and it were sucked up into the chimney. Then he turned on Mum. He were going to hit her in the face - hard - but I came between them.

'"And you, you little shit..." he shouted and he grabbed me by the throat and banged me up against the wall. I could hardly breathe but he was still squeezing.

'"Leave him alone!" My mum was screaming and she was holding the poker. "Let him go or I swear to God I'll crack your skull open even if I swing for it. LET HIM GO!"'

'He loosened his grip and I ran to Mum.

'"Right. That's it,' she said. 'I've had enough. I am packing a bag and we are leaving you. I will be seeing the solicitor about a divorce on Monday. I want you to get out for good. I don't want to find you here when I come back. And don't even think of trying to find us."

'"What about the kids?" he said. "They're my kids an' all."

'"You can forget about custody after that little scene. Ben's coming with me. Sandra's at her friend's for the weekend. I'll collect her. Don't you go anywhere near her or I will go straight to the police. Do you hear me? Now get out!"'

'Bloody hell!' I said again. There didn't seem anything else I could say.

'Too right,' Ben said. 'And do you know the worst thing about it?'

'Go on.'

'He were stone cold sober. He normally only freaks out like that when he's trollied.'

'Boys!' It was my mum calling up the stairs. 'Come here a minute.'

We went down.

'I want you to go and get Sandra from Barbara's,' she said. 'Don't alarm her. Keep it low key.'

'I'm sorry to be such a nuisance,' Mrs Westwell said to my mum. 'We've nowhere else to go.'

'Oh, nonsense, love. It'll be cosy. You'll see - and you're to stay as long as you need to - and that's that.

'Now, Stuart, we'll put Sandra and Auntie Teresa in the spare bedroom and Ben can go in with you. There's the Z-bed in the airing cupboard. Can you set it up for him? There's plenty of clean bedding in there.'

'Where's Dad?' I said.

'He's at the Rotary Club,' Mum said. 'He's going to get such a surprise when he gets home.'

And so he did. When he pushed open the living room door, he found his newly extended family eating cheese and biscuits and watching *Dr Finlay's Casebook*.

As we were getting ready for bed, Ben picked up one of the model battleships from the dressing table.

'Actually, these are pretty good,' he said. 'Some of these details look really fiddly.'

'Well, usually Tom does the assembly and I do the painting.'

'That must be pretty fiddly as well.'

'Well, yeah, it is sometimes.'

'Is this a frigate?' he asked.

'No, that's a destroyer.'

'Like me,' he muttered.

'What do you mean?'

'Oh nothing. Come on, you. Lights out. No talking.'

19.   SMOKE

THE WESTWELLS STAYED WITH US for the best part of three weeks and during that time Ben was on his best behaviour. He didn't play truant and he got up on time in the morning. We walked to school together, meeting Tom at the top of Brookhouse Lane. We had meals together and would watch telly together. He would even help me with the washing up after tea. Mum wouldn't hear of Sandra doing any chores and Ben would pull his best gargoyle faces at her behind the adults' backs.

He still had his football commitments but we were thrown together quite a lot. One evening he even joined Tom and me in putting together a Bristol Blenheim Bomber. Tom still came round for our syndicate homework sessions. Ben had different homework and worked on his own. I suspect that the time he spent with us at Whalley Range was the first time he actually completed his tasks since we first started at QEGS, and I'll bet when the Westwells returned home there was a sudden and total relapse.

Once, the three of us were sitting at the dining room table. Tom and I were translating some Latin. Ben sat apart with his head bowed and his fingers in his hair, huffing and puffing at some maths problem. I offered to help him and met with such a violent rebuff that I never offered again. We were an uneasy triangle, to be honest.

Mrs Westwell - I felt I was far too old to call her Auntie Teresa - went to see a solicitor a few days after they moved in with us. Mum went with her for moral support. I believe she was urged to report the assault to the police but she didn't want the fuss. At home, the grown ups kept having intense conversations, and Sandra, Ben and I were often sent upstairs or into the dining room. Frankly, I wasn't much interested.

It was quite good fun having Ben staying with us. He would say: 'Lights out - no talking' every night, but we would natter on for ages all the same. Even so, I didn't feel we'd regained the intimacy of our younger selves, though that didn't bother me particularly.

I did glean that the divorce wasn't going to be problematic. After three weeks, Teresa Westwell received a letter from her husband to say that he had moved out of the house for good and that she could return. It had been sent via the solicitor because Ben's dad had no idea where his family were living. Ben was sent round to Brookhouse Lane one weekend to check that the house was really empty. It was. Two days later the Westwells left our house and life returned to normal.

By normal, I mean it was very quiet. I missed having Ben around so much and, for the very first time, began to regret being an only child. I think I was also beginning to develop a crush on Sandra, who I thought was beginning to look quite sexy as she grew older. Of course, I didn't say this to Ben, knowing full well the blistering scorn he would pour on any such idea.

And, by normal, I also mean that the sense of distance between us re-established itself. Some days, I wouldn't see him in school at all, whether he was playing truant or not. Our form rooms were now upstairs in the Holden Laboratory building, and though they were in the same corridor, we came and went via different doors at either end.

During the February of 1964, there was a lot of flu around. It wasn't as bad as four years later in my first year at university but, all the same, there were a lot of absences and these were as bad among the staff as among the boys. With fewer masters around there was a distinct whiff of indiscipline about the place. It wasn't revolutionary but the chatter in Big School during morning assembly went on longer than usual as the masters entered. It took longer for boys to return to their form rooms after break. It took longer for classes to settle.

It became rather boring because absent masters meant boring written work and a cover teacher. At the peak of the crisis there was a severe shortage of staff to take lessons and, more than once, our entire year group was sent to an improvised 'silent study hall'. This was in the old huts, where our form rooms had been in the first year. It was a standing joke that the huts had been built in the Great War as a 'temporary measure'. And yet, there they still were, a long wooden building, baking in summer, freezing in winter and dusty all the year round. There was a stage at one end and four classrooms, all divided by movable partitions.

When the partitions were rolled back, you had a long open hall which could accommodate four forms together, and one master, seated at a desk on the stage, could see the whole year group - in other words, one member of staff could do the work of four. Cunning.

These sessions were ruled in a draconian way and, on the whole, the boys were compliant and the rule of silence was generally kept, though that's not to say there wasn't the occasional twanging ruler, or an obscene drawing being circulated.

One sleepy afternoon, I was seated near the back with something like eighty heads bowed down in front of me at their desks. 4A was at the back and 4D at the front below the master's dais. This implied correlation of academic ability with good behaviour was not necessarily a guarantee of peace. Since I became a teacher myself, I learned early on that a group of very bright kids can get up to more subversive devilry than their less able peers, who are too amiably dim to get up to much mischief.

Today, however, we were all docile. I could see Ben, whose white blond hair was very distinctive, sitting amongst his peers in 4D. He was at the side where the corridor ran.

I felt very drowsy. It was a cold day and paraffin heaters were breathing out their hot draughts here and there. They only provided pockets of warmth though. Those who were unlucky enough to be out of their range sat huddled in scarves and overcoats and even gloves. The fumes from the heaters made your eyes smart.

It was silent, or very nearly. There are some people who cannot put a pen down without a clatter. There are people who cannot sit still. And there were serial sniffers about. Anyone with the temerity to blow his nose would be greeted with exaggerated waves of tutting, which would subside when the master looked up and rapped his ruler on his desk.

I was almost nodding off when I became aware of a commotion on the window side, opposite the corridor, in the area where 4D were sitting. Grey smoke was seeping out from behind a tall wooden cupboard. Boys were getting up from their places and moving away, coughing.

By the time Mr Cunningham had come down from the stage, the smoke had increased in volume and was billowing into the room. He hit a fire alarm, grabbed a fire extinguisher and began to spray foam behind the cupboard. We knew what to do and started moving out.

'Leave your things!' Mr Cunningham shouted above the siren. 'No talking. Just go!'

There were four doors into the corridor and three exits into the top quad where the entire school was beginning to assemble at the far end by the old gym. I saw another couple of masters and the School Marshal running towards the huts.

This was wonderful.

As we stood in our form ranks in alphabetical order, as we had been trained to do, the buzz was phenomenal. If the huts had gone up in flames, it would have been like the Twilight of the Gods we had learnt about in music. The buildings were almost completely of wood and highly combustible. The entire fourth form could have been roasted like racks of Sunday joints. Mr Cunningham was the hero of the hour. He had saved us all from premature cremation. Mild-mannered Mr C was really Superman.

But how had it started? An electrical fault? That was the consensus among us until Mr Cunningham emerged with his colleagues and joined the group of staff in conference in front of the ranks of boys.

Dr Devereux, the Deputy Head, blew his Acme Thunderer whistle and there was immediate silence. Dr Devereux was terrifying. No boy who wished to keep his hide would defy the Acme Thunderer.

The Head began to speak. He commended the school on the efficient way it had assembled in response to the fire alarm, and the fourth form in particular for its speedy evacuation of the building. However, he said, it would appear that the fire had been started deliberately. A great deal of screwed up paper had been placed behind the cupboard. Some kind of home-made slow fuse had been employed. This was a very grievous situation.

There was a burst of chatter, quashed immediately by a burst from the Thunderer.

The Headmaster outlined his plan, and you had to admire how swiftly and efficiently it had been put together. The school was to return to classes immediately. The fourth form were to return to their form rooms. They would be supervised by prefects. Any misbehaviour would be treated severely. Fourth formers would be interviewed one by one by senior staff in Big School. They would be called by a prefect. After the interview, each boy should return to the Old Huts, which had been declared safe by the School Marshall, and resume private study.

The interviews were carried out pretty rapidly and we were called seemingly at random. None of the staff were forensic experts, of course, and I think, from what others said afterwards, that the questions had been standardised.

When my turn came, I was asked:

    Had I arrived early at the huts?

    Where was I sitting?

    Who had been sitting on either side of me?

    Who had been sitting in front of me?

    Did I see anyone acting suspiciously near the bookcase?

    Did I see or hear anything suspicious at all?

Had I heard anyone planning the event?

Had I heard any gossip about it?

I pointed out that since I was one of the last to arrive I wasn't much use to the enquiry. Mr Oliphant, who was my interrogator, seemed terribly bored if anything, and dismissed me quickly enough. I think he was resentful at losing a free period.

Ben arrived at Big School just as I was leaving. A prefect was stationed in the ante-room to prevent any communication.

He didn't see Ben give me a lewd wink.

20.   THE INQUISITION

I COULD SEE THE TREES. I'd always been able to see the trees. But at the time I couldn't see the wood.

I knew Ben was fascinated by fire but I didn't automatically link everything up. These pages are building into a narrative where certain conclusions about Ben will seem inevitable - with hindsight.

But hindsight, by definition, is not available when you're in the middle of events. It wasn't certain, in the middle of the last war, that the allies would win. No-one knew, when the British fleet sailed for the Falklands in 1982, whether the islands would be recaptured. It was unimaginable, when computers were the size of a house, that one day, a computer with vastly more power would fit into your pocket. Or that your current mobile phone has greater functionality than the computers that enabled man to land on the moon in 1969.

You cannot see the contours of things as they evolve, let alone their outcome. Life does not compose. You can't see the plot until it's all over.

What Ben's lewd wink meant, I wasn't sure. I am describing it as lewd because it had the racy cockiness of someone who had just got off with the best-looking girl in town. But did it mean that he had started the fire behind the bookshelves? Or did it simply signal that he was enjoying the disruption to the daily routine that the fire had caused? I wasn't so sure.

When I'd arrived Ben was at the other side of the room, some distance from the cupboard. It's true I'd arrived late and Ben was already there, but to have started the fire, he would have had to get there before anybody else. Either that, or he had accomplices. I couldn't believe that. If there had been others involved I thought the staff Gestapo must soon get to the bottom of it.

The Headmaster had said that the fire had been started deliberately. Again, I wasn't wholly convinced. That there had been a lot of paper behind the cupboard was no surprise to me, even then. Boys will do anything rather than *put* rubbish in the bin. Usually, they are more likely to throw it *at* the bin, preferably from a distance, in a kind of litter basketball. The top or back of a cupboard would do if it were nearer.

I am willing to bet that you would find litter down the back of any free-standing cupboard in any school in the land, just as I would bet big money that you would find masses of dried chewing gum under every table or desk in any classroom in the country, no matter how posh the school.

And what about this fuse? It would have to have been a slow-burning one, because it was a long time before Mr Oliphant arrived to supervise us and a while after that before the smoke began to appear. I had no idea how you made a slow burning fuse and I certainly had no idea how you would identify that one had been used. I thought you'd have to be an expert to do that, somebody from the Fire Brigade, for example. Come to think of it, why had they not been called? Was it some desire to protect the school's name?

Was it not more likely that the fire had been started by someone nearer the cupboards? And yet, wouldn't that be really stupid? Someone would be bound to see you in the crowded space and your proximity to the cupboard would put you amongst the prime suspects.

Another scenario that suggested itself to me was that a party of determined smokers might have been in there before the study session had begun. Such things were not unknown. Perhaps, they had been interrupted and chucked the butts behind the cupboard. Maybe one of them had not been properly extinguished.

But again, would Mr Oliphant and the School Marshal not have found the evidence?

Or was I just in denial, trying to protect my friend?

In the end, it made no odds. The Grand Inquisition found out nothing.

At assembly the following morning, Mr Devereux announced that, until further notice, boys would not be allowed into any classroom until their teacher arrived, and that they must wait in the corridors. In the event, this draconian rule was quietly repealed after a couple of days. Hordes of boys making a racket in the corridors was a remedy worse than the disease, and pupils who had been denied entry to their form rooms were often late for lessons in laboratories, or the art room or the gym.

Gradually, the excitement of The Great Fire ebbed and it was forgotten. The school returned to its routines. I saw less and less of Ben.

The A stream was a fast stream, which meant that we sat O levels after just four years. The other forms in our cohort took five years before they sat these exams. This meant that I entered the sixth form at the age of fifteen. Ben began the year in the upper fifth. Their form rooms were below stairs in the ivy-covered Radcliffe wing, where Geography was taught. The Arts

Sixth were in Hartley House with its lawns and the little cloistered quadrangle at the back of the science block. There was little incentive to leave this privileged little world except at lunch-times but, since lunch-times were staggered, I hardly ever saw Ben in school any more.

My sixth form subjects more or less chose themselves. I had done adequately in Maths and the science subjects and impressively in English and languages and so I chose to study English, French and German to A level. I was lucky that I was good at the subjects I liked. I had worked hard at the sciences but I was happy to say farewell. Tom went on to the science side but we remained friends out of school, and I had other friends in my classes, so the sixth form was a happy time for me.

However, this is Ben's story, not mine. I heard about him from time to time through the gossip machine. Halfway through my lower sixth year, I heard that he had left the school, whether of his own volition or because the school had had enough of him, nobody seemed sure. Apparently, he'd been accepted at St Peter's but again the rumours were vague.

A year later I heard on the grapevine that he had been expelled. The reasons given for this varied: theft, drunkenness, taking drugs (purple hearts), attacking a teacher. These all turned out to be spurious, as I discovered later. I don't believe he was expelled either: he just never turned up.

Another piece of gossip turned out not to be spurious after all, and I know this because the source was impeccable - my mum. She told me about it when I was 17 and in the Upper Sixth. Though Teresa Westwell was an infrequent visitor to our house on Whalley Range these days, Mum would often pop round to their house on Brookhouse Lane to see how she was. She appeared to be flourishing and was much happier without her bully of a husband. The divorce had gone through and the Westwells never saw him. It seems he was living with a barmaid in Darwen. Ben was a constant trouble to her, however.

Apparently, he'd got a girl 'into trouble'. This was, of course, a euphemism for getting her pregnant which was still considered to be a catastrophe. I had next to no sex education at home, and what I knew I'd gleaned from books from quite an early age. And I knew enough to know that much of what we saw on display in the cabinets in the waxworks in Blackpool was sensational rubbish. There was no sex education at school apart from a couple of dry lessons on the mechanics of reproduction in mammals which, were too boring even for sniggers.

I did have a special 'talk' from Mum about 'girls' when I was fourteen, which was hilariously late, of course. It boiled down to:

1.   Don't get too involved with any one girl
2.   Love 'em and leave 'em
3.   Be careful
4.   You could ruin your career
5.   If you got a girl in the family way, you'd be expected to marry her.
6.   You don't want to be shackled with a wife you don't love.
7.   You can't afford to be a father on a university grant

What 'be careful' meant precisely, she was too embarrassed to say, and I was too embarrassed to ask. I already knew, of course: rubber johnnies.

Mr Green, the barber, had been saying: 'Does sir require anything for the weekend?' since I was about eight. It was his only joke. In my innocence, I'd once said: 'I'd like a bike, please.' He'd regaled the waiting queue with this story every time I went in there until I went up to Cambridge. It became very tedious.

As for Ben, the thought of my friend having a child at seventeen - I couldn't take it in.

Who was the girl, I wondered.

21. CHANGING TIMES

IT TURNS OUT THAT THE GIRL WAS IRENE PIKE from Enamel Street. It was Ben himself who told me about it much later.

'She was nothing to look at,' he'd said, 'but she was easy.'

The Pikes were a big family whose house was across the back street from Ben's. The children were near feral, ragged and dirty-looking. I think there must have been about ten of them. Irene was the eldest and she at least took some trouble with her appearance and personal hygiene. Their father was a thug of a man who always wore a bib and braces and a collarless striped shirt. He always had a fag in the corner of his mouth. What he did for a living was unclear, but it was assumed that it was probably criminal in nature. His wife was a blowsy woman and the rumour was that she was on the game.

My mother's 'sex education' briefing, which I'd found almost comical at the time, suddenly seemed relevant.

Ben certainly had no intention of getting seriously involved with Irene, and his plan had certainly been 'to love her and leave her'. Their liaison had happened in the back street one night.

'Do you remember that anatomy exhibition in Blackpool?' he'd said to me. 'Well, I wasn't dead keen on getting a spaghetti willy so I thought it was time to stop being a virgin. Anyway, she egged me on.'

As for Mum's advice to be careful, that had gone by the board.

'You don't think about that stuff when you're worked up. Anyway, we hadn't planned to do it. I thought it were just a snogging session but we got carried away.'

When she missed a period they had both been very scared. In fact, Ben was terrified. What would they do when Irene began to show?

'Old Man Pike would have forced us to get wed,' Ben had said. 'If I refused, he'd have killed me. My God, fancy being spliced to Irene Pike for the rest of your life - all for the sake of a knee-trembler against the back door in the dark.'

Of course, Ben had no career to ruin at that point and certainly no plans to go on to university. All the same, he had the imagination to dread a future with no prospects.

I had very mixed feelings about all this when he told me about it.

'You were a cad and a bounder, sir,' I said to him, affecting the pompous tones of an affronted Victorian moralist. 'You should have been horsewhipped out of the parish.'

The trouble was that I really was shocked. It wasn't so much that he'd risked both their futures, but it was his cavalier attitude towards Irene that was so alien to me. Of course, I understood the urgency of the moment but couldn't quite grasp how he'd arrived at the moment in the first place - in a back alley with a girl he found unattractive and didn't respect. I thought back to our trespassing in the waxworks at Blackpool and all the ghastly exhibits that were designed to make sex terrifying, unless it were with a human being of the opposite sex within wedlock, in the missionary position, as infrequently as possible and for procreation only.

I thought back even further to the time when we were on the thrilling brink of puberty, and I had had to help Ben revise his entrenched view that you had to service your girlfriend at least once a month in order to *prevent* her from getting pregnant. He had believed that menstruation was proof that you'd been success-ful. I practically had to force him to read the entries on reproduction in *Encyclopaedia Britannica* in the Library, and even then his view seemed to be that the august reference books were out of date.

'Aye, but that were *then*, Stewpot,' he'd said, using the glass frontage of a display case in the entrance hall to comb his hair. 'Scientists know a lot more about sex nowadays than back then. One day soon, they'll be able to make babies in test tubes out of chemicals and you'll be able to buy them in shops.'

'And sex will stop altogether, you reckon?' I said.

'No, dumbo,' he replied. 'We'll all go to special clinics to get sterilised and then we can have sex all the time.'

Surely to God, Ben hadn't retained these outlandish views right up to his sad little adventure with Irene Pike? Of course not. He knew what was what. He'd used Irene Pike callously, hoping he would get away with it.

But Ben was my friend. Even though all this happened during a period of estrangement and I didn't learn about it until our paths began to run together again, Ben was my friend and I was loyal. Even though I never even thought about him from one week to the next, if someone had asked me if I had a best friend, I would have said: 'Yes, of course, Ben Westwell.'

So who was I to judge him? After all, though I knew a great deal about the theory and mechanics of sex, I knew less than nothing about girls. Our school was single sex at the time and since primary school I'd had little contact with girls at all. When I did encounter them, at parties organised by parents, for instance, I would be overcome with shyness and embarrassment. I just didn't know what to say and would be gauche, inept and prone to blushing.

Of course, I was an only child while Ben had a sister, even though they didn't get on. All the same, he was completely at his ease among girls and would soon have them giggling with his risqué jokes and his repertoire of gargoyle faces. And, of course, he was very good-looking.

No, he was more than completely at his ease - he was like a dog with two cocks.

As for me, it wasn't that I was queer or anything. I enjoyed the camaraderie of the all-male universe at school but I hadn't started fancying boys. My fantasies were 'normal', whatever that means, and my personal machinery was in working order, if you get what I'm saying. Actually my fantasies were quite vivid. It's probably best if I don't go into detail, but I remember having a powerful crush on Sandy Shaw and, later, Marianne Faithfull.

Strangely enough, my naivety and bashfulness were probably the norm amongst our peers and it was Ben's easy nonchalance that was the exception. Back then, 'good girls didn't'. Back then good girls 'saved themselves' for Mr Right and a church wedding. Good boys were told that it was important to get a foot on the ladder and think about a career. 'All that' could wait until later. At least, this was true of the middle classes to which my education had effectively elevated me.

Actually, I had a strong suspicion that sometimes good girls *did* and that good boys were only too happy to put their careers on hold when the chance presented itself. Unlike Ben, however, they were too savvy to get caught out. I began to suspect rather later that the boys and girls from the secondary moderns were banging like rabbits at every opportunity, and that that was the way things had always been through the ages. We grammar school boys were the oddity in our mono-sexual worlds where we strove for academic glory by suppressing the prickly turmoil in our trousers.

It was a socio-economic proposition really. If we could contain ourselves and live chastely behind the high walls of our Priory of Learning, we could acquire great riches, and great riches would surely lead, in turn, to fragrant females falling at our feet.

It was all a great capitalist scam, said Duncan Hempsall, the form's pet communist. A boy of twelve or younger is capable of fathering a child, Duncan would argue, but the capitalists won't let this happen. The boy must not produce children until he can afford to raise them. Infants must not be allowed to be a burden on the state.

This was wrong-headed, Duncan argued. The boy's biological nature is suppressed and his childhood artificially prolonged in order that he can preserve and promote 'the system'. I have to confess that I didn't know what he was on about most of the time but he carried you away with his passion, if not his logic. We approved of the idea that the authorities were denying us sexual autonomy, and were tempted towards revolution by Duncan's words of fire.

The other great sexual dragon he wanted to slay was the idea that boys were allowed, nay, expected to sow their wild oats, whereas any girl worth marrying should maintain her virginity. The rest were just tarts. Duncan said this was barbaric, bogus and medieval. I suppose he was a proto-feminist in our all-male enclave. He went on to read law at Oxford and is now an MP for a west country constituency.

When we went into the sixth form it was clear that, much as we admired Duncan's soap box oratory, our attitudes remained barbaric, bogus and medieval. All our conversation was about sex.

Actually, that's not literally true. We were pretty high-minded academically and had heated conversations about whether or not Marlowe was better than Shakespeare, and whether or not Bob Dylan was better than both. All the same, despite this juvenile iconoclasm, we would soon veer back to the fact that we were all still saddled with our virginity.

Apart from Alan Towers. Alan was a really nice lad - not particularly good-looking, not particularly bright, not particularly anything really, except that his background was difficult. He was brought up by a single mother and they were always hard up. His mother had two jobs in order to keep up a decent standard of living. You could tell that they were poor, if you were very sharp. Alan's trousers were tight and shiny, and only reached the top of his socks because his mum couldn't afford to replace them and he'd outgrown them. She couldn't afford the elaborate sixth form blazer badge either, and his jacket was plain black. It's to the credit of our school that no-one ever mentioned the relative poverty of kids like Alan - or

Ben and me for that matter. There was no bullying about it.

It was because Alan was so nice that no-one disbelieved him when he told us one break that he and his girlfriend had done 'it'. It was common knowledge that he had been going out with the same girl since they were twelve. It was no spur of the moment thing. They had actually planned it. Alan had bought condoms in Boots and they had fixed a date and time.

We were amazed. Unto us, he was suddenly like a god. So elevated had he become in our eyes that I remember thinking at the time how strange it was that he didn't look any different.

It was like crime really, but sweeter. All you needed was motive, means and opportunity. Well, we all had the motive and the means but the opportunities were rare. Parents were very much of a 'not under our roof' mentality back then. Because his mother was always out at work, Alan not only had the opportunity but the luxury of taking his girlfriend up to his bedroom for several hours of private pleasure.

Unlike Ben and his 'knee-trembler' in a back alley.

22.   THE JOINT PLAY READING SOCIETY

THE POET PHILIP LARKIN famously wrote:

> *Sexual intercourse began*
> *In nineteen sixty-three*
> *(which was rather late for me) -*
> *Between the end of the 'Chatterley' ban*
> *And the Beatles' first LP.*

Well, by contrast, 1963 was much too *early* for me, as was 1967 even, the year my friend Alan said goodbye to his chastity. That, incidentally, was the year that the Beatles' *Sergeant Pepper* came out and made a seismic difference to our tastes in music.

I remember the end of the 'Chatterley' ban, though. I was 13 at the time. It was on the news.

A reporter was interviewing furtive men in raincoats and prim ladies in hats queuing outside a London bookshop to buy it. They were full of feeble excuses like: 'It's for research purposes' and 'I'm getting it for a friend'.

Actually, Dad had a copy. He'd backed it with floral wallpaper which may have fooled Mum but it didn't fool me. He left it in the living room once and I had a good look, thumbing through it for the 'dirty' bits. They were hilariously bad, I thought. I put it back on Dad's chair just in time because he came in, picked it up, gave me a suspicious look, and disappeared.

The thing is, people talk about the Swinging Sixties but, in Blackburn at any rate, they didn't happen until the next decade. Sexual intercourse didn't begin for me until I was twenty and at university. For a good many people, and taking into account that people tend to lie about sex, it's my guess that that was pretty normal.

However, it was in the upper sixth that I began to cast off my shyness around girls and even acquire a girlfriend. I had the Joint Play Reading Society [French] to thank for that.

I still have my Year Book for 1967. This was a little booklet, bound in blue cloth, which contained everything a pupil needed for a fulfilling life at QEGS. There was a list of members of staff, school prefects and house prefects; times and venues for detentions (or Punishment School as it was rather dramatically called); there was a calendar of term dates and miserable homework timetables. Then there was a catalogue of extra-curricular clubs and societies, with a brief description and the names of staff presidents and pupil secretaries. Finally, there were many pages of sports fixtures.

The clubs were many and varied and I suppose the variety was a credit to the school: there were the Astrological and Meteorological Society, the Junior Chemical Society, the Chess Club, the Community Service Committee and the Christmas Card Club. This group of oddballs spent a year devising about six different designs for Christmas cards which went on sale in the Michaelmas Term, and very good they were. There was the Duke of Edinburgh scheme, the Elizabethan Debating Society, the Fencing Club and the Film Society, which showed films in Big School on winter evenings. This society had a charming offshoot called the Junior Projectionists Club. There were a Madrigal Society, a Printing Society, a Photographic Society, a Society of Change Ringers and a Stamp Club.

In amongst this frenzied activity I note entries for the Joint Play Reading Society [English] and the Joint Play Reading Society [French]. Despite their academic nature, these two societies were well-attended, and part of the reason for that lay in the word 'Joint'. It meant girls - Sixth Form girls from Blackburn Girls'

Grammar School. Sometimes we would meet in the Sixth Form Common Room in Hartley House at QEGS and sometimes at the Girls' School on Buncer Lane. For those of us of an academic bent, it was good value but mostly, despite their fierce chaperone, Mrs Bradley, it was about girls. Mrs Bradley wore tweeds and had a face like a potato and buttocks to match.

I was a member of both branches of this association. This is what my Year Book says about the French Branch:

Joint Play Reading Society [French]
President: Mme S Laspougeas
Secretaries: Stuart Cooper; Sandra Westwell
The society exists for the reading and exploration of French Dramatic Literature from Racine and Corneille to Anouilh and Sartre.

To see Ben's sister's name there in print after all these years gives me a strange twinge. What our duties were as secretaries, I no longer remember. I seem to recall that we had to select and borrow sets of the play texts from Blackburn Public Libraries. I think that was it. Anyway, it brought us together outside of school and it was not too long before we were going out together.

I don't think Ben ever knew about this. I hadn't seen him for nearly two years and I wouldn't have told him anyway. I'm sure Sandra never told him either. He'd got in with a bad bunch in Bolton, she said, and was never at home these days. When he was, she avoided him.

Sandra was lovely. I'd fancied her for ages but by now she was really fit. I earned a lot of kudos among my mates when I started going out with her. She had lots of Ben's good qualities without the downsides. And she was really bright - ambitious too. I couldn't help thinking that Ben was just as clever and wondering what he could have achieved if he were not so lazy and contrary.

Her French was fluent and her accent pretty authentic. Actually mine wasn't bad. There's a view that northerners have an advantage in learning French because the mouth is more mobile when you speak in a northern accent. I don't know if that's true but it's certainly plausible. Anyway, Sandra wanted to live and work in Paris - any old job would do, so long as she could immerse herself in the lifestyle.

We weren't together long - probably not much more than two months - but I was happy while it lasted. We saw *Cat Ballou, Taras Bulba* and *Sink the Bismarck* at the QEGS film society and *Bonnie and*

Clyde and *The Graduate* at the Odeon. We had a day trip to Manchester and saw *A Midsummer Night's Dream* at the Royal Exchange. We climbed Pendle Hill with a group of friends on a dull day, and a sudden burst of sunshine revealed the patchwork fields of Lancashire spread out below us with ribbons of mist floating over them. We sat for hours over long-emptied coffee mugs in the steamy atmosphere of the Wimpy Bar on Northgate, talking about literature, France and the future.

We never met at her house, perhaps because of an unspoken unwillingness to bump into Ben, even though he was hardly ever there. We never went to my house either. I was sure Mum would want to marry us off.

Sandra was one of the good girls. We spent quite a lot of time mooching around Corporation Park and kissing - romantically rather than passionately. Once, in the Essoldo, opposite the Town Hall, she allowed me to, what the bad boys call 'cop a feel'. The film was *Witchfinder General*. It was violent and quite scary, I suppose, though I've never been able to take anything with Vincent Price in it very seriously. During a scene in which a priest was being tortured by having needles put into his back, Sandra snuggled up close to me in the dark. I could smell her hair. Cautiously, I stroked her arm and moved my hand to her breasts. She did not resist.

But when I tried to put my hand inside her jumper, she gently but firmly moved it, sat up and leaned away. Not long afterwards, she dumped me.

'Is it because...?' I said, thinking perhaps that I'd been too forward too fast.

'No, nothing like that,' Sandra said. I was quite impressed by the way she seemed to be able to intuit what I was thinking.

'Is there somebody else then? Is that what it is?'

'No, there's nobody else,' Sandra said, and she gave me a quick peck on the cheek.

'What is it? What have I done wrong?'

'Nothing. Oh, Stewpot, don't look so miserable. It's really nothing to do with you at all. I just don't want to be tied down at the moment. I want to concentrate on my work.'

'Boys can wait, is that it?'

'More or less. We can still be friends.'

And with that terrible little cliché our sweet little affair came to an end.

I am not going to lie and claim that I descended into rage, self-pity and madness. I was sad for a while and felt a bit empty but I would live. In any case, I was getting rather fed up with Mum saying every few minutes: 'What's the matter, love? You seem a bit down.'

And Sandra had a point. I was ambitious too and needed to get on with my academic work. My French teachers, Mr Frost and Mme Laspougeas were encouraging me to apply for Oxbridge, and I was keen. I went into overdrive. I read Balzac and Victor Hugo, I listened to French radio and read French magazines and newspapers. I acquired a French pen friend from Nantes called Paulette. She proved to be rather dull but I did learn quite a lot of teenage slang from her. I did think of asking Sandra if she wanted to meet up for French conversation practice but, fearing a rebuff, I didn't bother.

In the end, I did fine. I applied to St Stephen's College, did a term in third year sixth form, was called for interview and was accepted. I would go up to Cambridge the following October. Until then I had nine months to fill. The college sent me a formidable reading list which would occupy me, but I also wanted to make and save some money. I needed a job.

Just before Christmas Sandra rang me. She said she had some good news to share. We agreed to meet up for a drink at the Clarence in the shopping precinct. The pub was still quite new and had the plush feel of a good hotel bar.

Sandra was buoyant. She had gained a place at Oxford and was deferring for a year. In the meantime she had secured a post as *au pair* with a wealthy family in Toulouse. She would have a smart self-contained flat at the top of a huge house in the Bauhaus style. Her charges would be two boys aged eight and ten and she would also be expected to teach them English. She had been interviewed in London and had been introduced to the family. She declared the boys 'enchanting'.

There was also a swimming pool.

'From Brookhouse Lane to this!' she said. 'Haven't we done well?'

I raised my pint of Thwaites bitter and said: 'To us!'

'To us!' Sandra replied.

And, in the New Year, Sandra passed out of my life.

Shortly afterwards, Ben blazed back in.

23.   THE NORTH WEST ELECTRICITY BOARD

I FOUND MYSELF A JOB at the North West Electricity Board at Whitebirk as a temporary clerk. The advert was in *The Lancashire Evening Telegraph* and it said the post was for a year but I applied anyway. When I was called for interview, the Senior Clerk, who was a very pleasant, very tall man with a comb-over and matching tie-pin and cufflinks, said that nine months would be fine, and when could I start. Immediately, I said, and was told to report to Mr Vole at eight o'clock the following Monday. Wages would be £8.15s.6d a week.

'There's another young lad from QEGS starting in a couple of weeks' time,' the Senior Clerk said. 'You'll probably know him. I forget the name just for the moment.'

This was intriguing but I was so excited about my début in the world of work that it soon slipped out of mind. I offered to pay my parents rent but Mum said I could keep my earnings if I started to buy some of my own clothes. Dad agreed but insisted I save some of the lolly, which I wanted to do anyway, and he said he would double anything I saved until I went up to Cambridge - which was obviously a brilliant incentive.

Mr Vole was a very small man with a very big moustache. It was very uneven and the whiskers seemed to be at random lengths. I thought he was aptly named because he resembled an escapee from *Tales of the Riverbank*. He had horn-rimmed glasses which seemed too big for his face and wore short-sleeved shirts and an oatmeal coloured waistcoat.

I don't think Fred Vole was an unkind man but he was a self-important kind of rodent and when he learned that I had a place at Cambridge he went out of his way to make sure I knew my place. I was put to work on filing.

In an age before computers, you have no idea how much paperwork a big concern like the NWEB generated. The organisation covered a large part of northern Lancashire and was concerned with the sales, maintenance and repair of appliances, both domestic and industrial, and with faults in supply. There were requisition forms, delivery notes and invoices with their top copies, blue copies, and yellow copies, reports and correspondence. These all had their proper places for storage and retrieval. A series of bays containing tiers of hanging files ran the whole length of the open plan office and covered every address in the region. There were standing cabinets for different kinds of paperwork, wooden index card boxes, and Rolodex rotators. Finally, there was what Fred referred to as WPB for any document which had become obsolete.

Each morning I would be presented with a basket of undifferentiated sheets of paper in different sizes and colours, and it was my job to find the right home for them. Once I'd been shown the various storage systems, it was easy. If you knew these destinations and the alphabet, no other brain power was required. It was, however, desperately dull.

Against his more officious nature, Fred was forced to admit to a measure of respect for my efficiency, though he did say at one point: 'Not bad, Cambridge, but don't work so fast. You don't want to put somebody out of a job.'

All the same, I was promoted. For a couple of hours a day I manned the phones in the Faults Department. I enjoyed this because it required a certain amount of diplomacy. Most of the time, it was simply a factual matter: listen, record details of the problem (on paper, of course) and pass the request on to the appropriate channel, usually Fred Vole. Fred would assess the urgency of the request and the task would be put on the engineers' worksheets. If it was an urgent matter, the job would be passed on to the engineers by radio.

Diplomacy was needed when callers were distressed or angry. I became pretty good at defusing these situations, and if you were distraught that the oven element of your Belling 335WH had failed and the hotpot you had been cooking for your husband's tea wouldn't be ready, I would be the one to talk to. Although I couldn't promise you that an engineer would call before the following day, I could reassure you that the hotpot would keep till then, and for tonight, how about the chip shop?

You didn't have to wait half the morning for me to pick up and you didn't have to go through a maze of menus when I did. As soon as I'd finished on one phone, I'd pick up the other and you'd be through to a real human being: me, the housewives' friend.

But I'm getting a bit ahead of myself.

On my second Monday morning at work, I was on filing duty when I noticed, at the other side of the office, the Senior Clerk talking to Ben. It seemed rather weird to see him in this context. He looked very smart with a neat back and sides, clean white shirt, fashionable sage green knitted tie and a blue serge suit.

After a while, the boss brought him over to a bay where I was sitting on the floor, filing documents in the rank that went from Laburnum Road to Larkhill. I noticed that Ben's shoes were highly polished, which was unusual to say the least.

'Now then,' the Senior Clerk said, 'do you two know each other?'

Ben pulled a grinning gargoyle face that the Senior Clerk was not meant to see.

'Slightly,' Ben said, winking.

'Very good,' the Senior Clerk said. 'Stuart, I would like you to initiate Ben into the mysteries of the filing system and then...erm...well, we shall see.'

And he wandered off on a tour of his domain, hands clasped behind his back like the late Duke of Edinburgh.

It was as if Ben and I had never been apart. Though Fred frowned on too much chatter unrelated to work, we were clever enough to be discreet and when we were in the document bays we were semi-secluded and it hardly mattered anyway.

After lunch, Ben was taken off by the Senior Clerk to learn the other roles associated with his position as Office Junior. One of these was to acquire and deliver supplies to the various departments, principally stationery. He had a trolley and would deliver typing paper, carbon paper, typewriter ribbons, Tipp-ex, pens, pencils, erasers, ink pads, date stamps, rubber bands, paper clips, staplers and staples in return for a properly entered requisition slip.

His other major role was as Post Boy. He had to sort the morning post and deliver it to the appropriate departments and, in the late afternoons he had to weigh and frank all outgoing letters and parcels ready for collection by the Royal Mail van at 4.45 pm on the dot.

The franking machine was in the typing pool which was partitioned off from the rest of the office, the party wall being made of wood panelling up to waist level with glass panels above. The reason for the partition was to seal off noise.

The rattle of ten machines and their carriage bells was pretty formidable in itself, but the girls themselves often made an unholy racket. There would be periods of intense concentration and then there would suddenly be an outburst of wild chatter and hysterical laughter. The Senior Clerk, whose desk was just in front of the typing pool, would rise from his plush swivel chair and glare through the window. The manic shrieking would subside to muffled giggles and eventually sink to concentration again.

I say 'girls' but there was quite an age range. The head of the pool was perhaps fiftyish and there was a teenage trainee, but most of them were in their thirties. They took a shine to Ben from the start. They would greet him with 'Hiya Gorgeous' or 'Hello Sexy' and their chatter would be full of innuendo. From time to time they would attempt to 'debag' him. Fred once sent me in there with letters to be typed, and there was Ben on the floor by the franking machine with his trousers round his ankles.

'They couldn't help themselves,' he said, pulling his kecks up over his Y-fronts and tucking in his shirt.

'He didn't struggle very hard,' said one of the girls.

'You're next,' another girl said to me.

'He has a nice bum, Stuart has,' another one said.

I think Ben liked all this.

I wasn't so sure that I did.

24.   FRIDAY NIGHTS

FILING WAS LESS TEDIOUS with Ben around and the days passed quickly.

Soon I was promoted again and spent part of each day operating the radios. This meant passing on information to the engineers out at work in the Board's vans, giving out jobs as instructed by Fred or helping with locations, using maps on the wall of the radio room. The vans were code-named 'Cherries' and I would contact them by saying, for instance: 'Base A to Cherry 3 - come in please.' This was great fun, and I think Ben was slightly jealous.

I got to know the men quite well. They were a genial lot and there was plenty of banter. There were funny stories too. There was the time Bill Owens was fixing a boiler while the owner popped out to the shops. He was trapped in the utility room by a large bulldog which wouldn't let him out. It just stood in the doorway looking grim and, whenever he moved, it started snarling and slavering. Then there was the time Jack Tierney was sent out to a lady who claimed that the hobs on her cooker weren't working, and when he arrived the appliance turned out to be a gas stove.

We looked forward to Fridays. Just before lunch, Freda from Accounts would come round with a tray bearing little brown paper envelopes with holes punched in the back and a cellophane window at the front. I could see that my first ever pay packet contained a blue fiver, three green pound notes, a brown ten bob note and some coins. It doesn't sound much, but I reckon it would be worth something like £130 now. With my first wage, I bought a smart blue sports jacket from Gray's and *Rubber Soul* by The Beatles from Reidy's music shop, and then opened a savings account at the Post Office.

At lunchtime on Fridays, after we'd been paid, the younger members of staff trooped along to the Red Lion at Whitebirk for pie and chips with gravy. At first, I just had a half of Lion bitter with my pie in case Fred Vole smelled beer on my breath, but when Ben joined us we upgraded to pints and got away with it.

During the last hour on Friday afternoon, Ben and I were allotted a special job. We were given the week's copies of *The Lancashire Evening Telegraph* and a mint copy of *The Blackburn Times,* which came out weekly. Our task was to scour every page for any reference to the North West Electricity Board, positive or negative. We had to cut out anything we found and paste the cutting in a scrapbook which was then passed to the Senior Clerk, who would decide if any action needed to be taken.

There was rarely anything much. There might be a grumble on the letters page or news of a new office opening in Ramsbottom, or an advert for a Hotpoint twin-tub, available at your NWEB showrooms. Hardly very exciting, but we could both skim-read pretty quickly, so during the last half hour of the week, Ben would catch up with his beloved Blackburn Rovers in the sports pages and I would do the crossword.

Ben and I took to going out on a pub crawl on Friday nights. Ben was staying at his Auntie's up Dunoon Drive in Shadsworth. He said his mother couldn't put up with him any more and the constant friction between him and Sandra was driving her bananas. His Auntie Helen was younger and much more indulgent.

We both had a bit of a trek to get home. We'd zoom off in opposite directions, have a quick tea, beautify ourselves, catch a bus into town and meet up by Queen Victoria's statue on the Boulevard.

It might surprise you to know that back then you wore a shirt and tie on a night out. Hard to believe that only a year later, we would be wearing flared trousers, grandad vests, and our hair would be below our ears. For now I wore my new sports jacket and Ben had a high-buttoned suit in emulation of The Beatles. Nor were there wine bars heaving with young-sters. No, we went on a pub crawl just like the grown ups.

We might start off right there at the Adelphi near the station, then on to the White Bull with its older clientele, and then the Little Bull, which had a great juke box and was thronged with young people. And fi-nally over to the Fleece for a bit of quiet and a good natter.

Or we would catch a bus out to Lammack and the Hare and Hounds near to the school's playing fields - a bit posh that - up to the Sportsman's at Four Lane Ends, over the famous 'Revidge Run', including the Dog Inn and the Corporation Park and then down to the Quarryman's and the Alexandra behind the school, which I'd used illicitly on the odd lunch-time when I was a sixth-former.

There were roughly five hundred pubs in Black-burn in those days and sometimes we would just get a bus at random and crawl our way back to town. Each pub had a distinctive character, from chintzy and twee with carpets and Toby jugs, through sporty with trophies and horse brasses, to bare-floored and basic. We'd play the one-armed bandits and the juke boxes, have a game of darts, or play snooker or table football. More often than not we just talked.

We would end up on the 'Barbary Coast'. Where this was exactly was open to dispute: some said it included the pubs on Mincing Lane. We took it to mean the trio of pubs which included the Peel, the Vulcan and the Jubilee. These pubs had a reputation for rough stuff. They were packed, noisy and full of smoke and the juke boxes were loud. There was always the tang of possible danger in the air, but to be honest I think that was part of the appeal. We only ever witnessed one fight. There was the sound of broken glass and a scream, and the crowd moved away from the two lads who were scrapping over a girl. The landlord threw them out on to the street double-quick, where the fight carried on, with other lads joining in and girls egging them on. Ben moved to join in but I pulled him away by the collar of his jacket.

We would end up buying battered sausages and chips at the Hake Boat on Salford before heading back to our buses. We dredged the chips with salt and vinegar, which soaked into the newspaper they were wrapped in. Then I would catch the number 14 bus home and Ben the 48 to Shadsworth.

I loved the novelty of getting drunk with Ben. I suppose we swilled quite a lot but we were young and could take it. We laid off the spirits and stuck to beer so we never got dizzy drunk or vomity drunk. It was good to be young and to own the future.

It was during these nights that Ben filled in for me what he'd been up to since he left school. He'd not lasted long at St Wilfred's. He was considered for the first team at football but was told he wouldn't be allowed to play for the school unless he buckled down with his academic work.

'Well, stuff that for a start,' he said to me. 'What kind of a bargain is that? It's nowt better than blackmail. They shouldn't trade off one against the other. I'm crap at Maths and English but brilliant at football, and they tell me I can't play unless I do my sums and write stories. What? It doesn't make sense, that doesn't. I could have been signed up for the Rovers by now if it hadn't been for that load of rubbish. So I stopped going.'

'Didn't you do your O levels, then?'

'Nah, waste of time. Anyway, I were fifteen by then. I didn't have to stay at school. I could get a job. Mum played Hamlet with me and said I were throwing my future away, a bright lad like me, but she had no idea how bored I was. It were doing my head in. It were like being in prison. Same old rubbish day in day out.

'Mind you, there were one bright thing at that school - the lasses. There were some smashers, I'm telling you, Stewpot. Skirts up to their knickers and knockers bursting out of their blouses. I used to skive off regular with a couple of them. We'd register and then slope out to the Boulevard and catch a bus to Accrington out of the way. Then we used to sit in the Blue Dahlia café all day. I miss that.'

He said that it was around this time that he'd got Irene Pike pregnant.

'I'm telling you, Stu, Old Man Pike would have turned me into scrag end if he'd found out. He's like a Mafia boss in Brookhouse, he is. Everybody's scared of him. They say his bodyguards have bodyguards. If he'd found out that I'd put his precious daughter in the pudding club, he'd have turned me into hotpot, no doubt about it.

'We kept quiet about it for a couple of months. We were terrified that she'd begin to show and then the game would be up. I'd be for the butcher's block and Irene reckoned she'd be put in a home until the baby was born, and then they'd take it from her and put it up for adoption. Even the thought of it had her skriking her eyes out. It did cross my mind to say that there was no proof that it was mine, but I'm not a complete shit. I couldn't do that.

'We had nobody to turn to, Stuart. Nobody.'

'What about your mum?' I said.

'Yeah, well, we thought of that but I wasn't exactly flavour of the month at the time and the thought of our Sandra sneering and gloating was a right no-no. She's in France now and she's got a place at Oxford when she comes back. Did you know that?'

'No,' I lied and then faltered. 'Well, I'd heard rumours.'

'She'll be looking down her nose at Her Majesty the Queen before long, that one,' Ben said.

I could hardly point out that the Sandra I knew was nothing like this slur. Obviously Ben's animosity came from a deep-seated resentment at being outshone by his younger sister. But I wasn't going to take sides - and she'd dumped me after all, so I ignored it.

'What happened?'

'Oh, she just got ridiculously good A levels, had an interview and they offered her a place on the spot.'

'No, not Sandra, you prannock, Irene.'

'Well, we thought about an abortion - but not for long. We couldn't go to her doctor. We didn't know anybody who'd do it and we could hardly ask around. We weren't keen on breaking the law anyway. And I didn't want to put her through it, if you want to know the truth. I might be a callous bugger sometimes but I drew the line at that.

'Besides, there was no way I could have afforded it. Mind you, there was no way I could afford the maintenance on a baby either. I was shafted, mate. Up Poop Creek without a paddle in sight.'

'What did you do? Did she have the baby?'

'No, mate, she didn't.'

'What happened?'

'What happened? I got lucky.'

25.   BEN'S CV

'WHAT DO YOU MEAN, you got lucky?' I said.

'She miscarried.'

'And that's lucky?'

'Yeah, it was lucky. What's your problem?'

'Lucky for you, you mean.'

'Obviously, but there was no way we could have brought up a baby properly. It was horrible and messy and she was in pain for a couple of weeks, but it was for the best.'

'How is she now?'

'I dunno. I haven't seen her since. Can we change the subject?'

I knew Ben well enough not to press it. He had always been inclined to clam up where his own emotions were involved. And I remember thinking that perhaps he was not being as cold-hearted as he appeared. The miscarried child was his too, after all. As ever, rightly or wrongly, I gave my friend the benefit of the doubt.

During our pub circuits, he continued to fill me in on what he had been doing since he quit school. He had tackled a number of dead end jobs. The first had been as a bottle washer in Thwaites' soft drink unit.

'My God, it was boring,' he said. 'Most of the time, I just unloaded the crates of empties and fed them into the bottle-washing machine. It could flush out light stuff like fag ends. Anything else I had to fish out by hand with a twisted wire thing. You would never believe what people stuff into empty pop bottles: pebbles, snotty hankies, dead wasps, rolled-up beer mats, slugs, and condoms, lots of condoms. Why? I mean, why? I tried imagining what kind of scenario would end up with you putting a used condom into a tonic water bottle?'

'Spare me the details,' I said.

'Never drink straight from a bottle,' he said. 'You wouldn't if you'd seen what I've seen.'

Actually, I took his advice. Years later, when it became fashionable to drink beer straight from the bottle in the American fashion, I remembered, and would always ask for a glass.

'Sometimes,' Ben went on, 'if they were short-staffed, they'd put me on the bottle-washing machine itself. It was a monster. You stood on a high platform and crates of empties rolled up to you and you fed the bottles upside down into the machine. Jets of really hot water would whoosh into the bottles and they'd disappear inside. Then they would come snaking out the other end in single file and the conveyor would take them to automated machines which would squirt syrup and carbonated water into them. Another robot would push crown caps on them. When they reached the end of the line, they'd be packed into crates and shunted into the store or sometimes straight on to the lorries.

'There might be a batch of dry ginger ale and then a batch of tonic water or bitter lemon. There'd be a pause while they changed the feed lines from a gallery where the sugar and syrups were mixed and you'd be standing there in clouds of steam, waiting. You could have a natter with the women who usually worked the washer, and that was all right.

'But otherwise, Stewpot, it was so blooming boring I were going doolally. You cannot even begin to imagine how bloody boring it was. So I jacked it in.'

'Then what did you do?' I said.

'I sat on my bum for a few weeks but that was boring as well, and my Auntie Helen was going mental at me. And I had no money at all so I got a job at a foundry near Bank Top. I made cores for bearings.'

'What's that when it's at home?' I said.

"Right. You put cores made of compressed sand into moulds before you pour the hot metal into them.

Then, when it's cold you smash the core and brush it out and you've got a core-shaped hole in your bearing.'

'How do you make them?'

'You have a machine with two hot metal plates with core-shaped indentations. You press a lever and the two plates come together; sand feeds in from a hopper above the machine, and compressed air is blasted in from underneath. You throw the lever again and the plates come apart and there's your core. You have to wear asbestos gloves to take it out. You have to keep the plates clean and well-oiled or the core will crumble and stick and it's a hell of a job to clean off bits of burnt core. You can feel the heat through your gloves but you have to get on with it or any future cores you make will be damaged and rejected. It was a nightmare from the start.

'The only good thing about it was when they actually poured the metal. The core shop was round the corner from the foundry itself but I used to go and watch during my breaks. They tipped a huge crucible out of the furnace and the molten metal ran in channels into the moulds. It was glorious. I would have liked to do that, but it was heavy work and pretty dangerous.

'Aluminium was best. Think of the pinkest thing you know: peaches, salmon, bubblegum, flamingoes -

well. It's pinker than that. And it glows. It runs down the channels with sparks flying off it and it's so dazzling you can't look at it for long.

'There was nothing dazzling about my job, though. It was even more boring than bottle-washing. Just one lever operation, repeated again and again. And I was swizzed about the money an' all.'

'How come?' I said.

'It was piece work.'

'What's that?'

'Well. They told me I could earn up to twelve quid a week, but they didn't explain that there was a pitiful basic rate of pay and the rest would depend on how many boxes of cores I made. I'd be paid *pro rata* for these.

'Jesus, I never even reached my quota. I was lucky to come away with much more than a fiver.'

'Why? Were you crap at it?'

'Probably, but that wasn't it. Some of the men were determined to make sure I didn't make the grade. When the charge hand, Donald, found out that I'd been at the Grammar he was pretty nasty about it. He used to say things like: "Be careful you don't get your hands dirty, pretty boy."

'He was in charge of dishing out the asbestos gloves. When mine were getting thin at the fingertips, making the job painful as well as tedious, he would say: "There's a couple of weeks' worth more work in them gloves, sweetie. Back to work now and don't cry."

'Don't get me wrong. Most of the men were fine but there were just a few bastards who had it in for me. It all came to a head one day when they put lumps of broken core into my sand hopper during the dinner break. When I came back for the afternoon shift the broken core worked its way into the feed pipe until it formed a blockage. Then, when I let in the compressed air, there was an explosion and the entire contents of the hopper blew up all over the shop floor.

'"You can clear that up, for a start, you gormless little snot-rag," Donald said, holding out a brush. "You're not making any more cores till you sweep up every speck of that sand."'

'Why didn't you tell him you'd been sabotaged?' I said.

'Do you think he'd have believed me?' Ben said. 'And besides, he were probably involved himself.'

'What did you do?' I said.

'I thrust the brush back at him,' Ben replied. '"Do it yourself," I said. "And you can stuff your job where the sun don't shine, you creep. You're nothing but a tinpot bully, Donald. I'll be in on Friday to pick up my wages."'

'Good for you,' I said. 'And what did he say?'

'He were right gobsmacked. All he could think of to say was: "You'll not be picking up much brass. Not at the rate you work."

'"Yeah well, I've been working a week in hand," I said, "so I'm owed summat. Enjoy your sad life, you sour-faced git." And I walked straight out.'

'I bet that felt good,' I said.

'Good? I walked out of that place on air, pal.'

'I'm proud of you, kid,' I said.

'So you should be,' Ben replied.

Looking back, I'm not sure how proud I really was.

26.   CHRISTMAS POST

WHEN BEN AND I WERE in our teens, they 'ripped the heart out' of Blackburn. From 1962 onwards, the centre of town as we had known it as children was razed to the ground. The old market on the cobbles by the town hall with its masses of tarpaulin-covered stalls disappeared. The built-up area between Victoria Street and Ainsworth Street was gutted and some dignified buildings were crushed, along with the slums. Shops, pubs, offices and homes were flattened by the bulldozer and the wrecking ball.

The new build didn't start immediately and for a while the whole centre of the town was a wasteland. However, during the decade, a brave new world gradually arose from the rubble. A covered market with a vast curved roof emerged alongside a new market hall with a café in the gallery. These wonders contained all the familiar stalls and even a bright new fish market. The complex stretched from Salford to Regent Street and was contained between Ainsworth Street and Penny Street.

From the Town Hall to Lord Street, an even more striking wonder came into being - an American style shopping mall, complete with plate glass shop fronts, supermarkets, and fountains. It wasn't known as The Mall at the time, although I believe it is now. For no reason I've ever been able to find out, it was known as 'The Precinct'. On top of the shopping centre was a multi-storey car park. Blackburn had entered the modern era.

There was much weeping and wailing and gnashing of teeth from the older generation about this 'wanton vandalism'. The 'Clowncil' [sic] had 'ripped the heart' out of the town, the elders said. They had destroyed Blackburn's heritage, they said. They had sacrificed the dignity of tradition with flashy banality. They had robbed the town of its character.

The apotheosis of their lamentations came with the demolition of the Market Hall clock. The Market Hall had already been knocked down and the clock tower stood alone above the débris for a week or so. A crowd gathered to see its final moments. The clock itself had already been removed and put into storage - in Manchester, I think. There were tears and cries of outrage as the roof with its time ball and the top quarter of the tower were toppled to the ground. Within an hour, there was only rubble.

'A filthy deed has been done today,' my dad said when he saw the photograph in the *Lancashire Evening Telegraph*. He could be quite pompous on occasion.

I should say something about the time ball. This was on a pole at the top of the tower. At noon a mechanism raised it up the pole and at one o'clock precisely, the ball dropped to its resting position and a gun was fired. Quite why, I don't know. I never actually saw the ritual. I now realise it was intended to copy the time ball on the Royal Observatory at Greenwich. The Observatory lies on the meridian and it was a reference point for shipping, not only in the Thames but throughout the world. You don't get much shipping in Blackburn, of course.

Anyway, in the second week of December, 1964, the time ball dropped for the last time and by the end of the month, it had all gone.

I felt sad about this and could empathise with the grief of the elders. The Market Hall and the Town Hall further along King William Street were imposing and architecturally interesting, even though both buildings had been blackened by the smoke of the Industrial Revolution. The Town Hall still stands, of course, in its Italianate grandeur and, since it was sandblasted to its original whiteness, I don't think it would look out of place in the principal piazza of a town in Tuscany or Lombardy. To be honest, I feel more nostalgic about the old town as it was, now that I am an elder myself.

It might look quaint and enchanting in old photographs but to be honest, the old market was not really such a gem. As a younger kid, I used to go shopping with Mum and she appreciated this because I could help carry bags back to Brookhouse Lane. She would treat me to a mug of cocoa or hot Bovril in Woolworths. When it rained, which in Blackburn is often, you risked cold water from the edge of the tarpaulins running down the back of your neck, or slipping on a cabbage leaf on the wet cobbles. The stalls were very close to each other and on such days it was quite unpleasant to be jostled by damp bodies. To have a wet umbrella come into contact with your bare leg - we wore shorts back then until we were twelve or thirteen - was very unpleasant indeed.

When it was all completed and up and running, Ben and I were very much in favour of the new Blackburn. How much nicer to stroll into the new market, wafted in by the savoury smells of meat and potato pies, cheese and onion pies and apple turnovers. Then there was the salty pong of fish and then the earthy aromas of fresh fruit and vegetables and banks of flowers. All the same old stalls were there, only there was more space between them and it was all under cover. Right in the middle was Walsh's sarsaparilla stall. A glass of this black, fragrant nectar ("Cools the Blood") was a must on Saturday mornings and, later perhaps, a milkshake in the Palatine Dairies café.

Ben and I liked the footbridge over Ainsworth Street which led from the Precinct to a spiral staircase inside a drum-like structure. I believe it was called the 'rotunda'. At its foot was the brand new St John's Tavern, replacing the old dive behind the church. We would sometimes start our Fridays there. In those days it was quite plush and comfortable and sold an excellent pint of Thwaites' bitter. We would lounge in the lounge bar and reminisce about our days as choristers as if they were a century ago.

Sometimes we would give the Barbary Coast a miss and end our Friday in the Ying Kin. This was a Chinese restaurant at the end of the new market complex, and wholly unlike its previous incarnation in rather rundown premises on Ainsworth Street, next to the Royal Cinema. It was on the first floor and vast windows looked out on to the night lights of Salford, the Old Bull and the Little Bull and up Railway Road to the Station. The floor space seemed infinite with acres of tables spread with pristine white tablecloths. Large potted plants seemed to breathe the exoticism of the Orient. It was almost too posh for Blackburn. We thought ourselves metropolitan.

After an evening of swilling beer, we would scoff down tongue-stinging yellow curries, served within rings of white rice, adding soy sauce because it was on the table and we thought that was what you did. Then we would eat lychees with ice cream, and, even though Ben called them 'blind man's eyeballs', I was not put off. Their strangeness made them delicious.

Ben continued to fill me in with the jobs he'd had since leaving school.

'Last year I did the Christmas post,' he said. 'They take people on during the build-up to the big day, mostly students. Not for yours truly tramping the streets in rain, hail and sleet. Oh no! Because I know my alphabet, they put me on sorting. You get a bit of a sore arm but I loved it. In would come the posties, cold and wet, with pink noses, to collect letters and packets for their next shift, whilst I expanded my geographical knowledge in the warmth.

'There are cubby holes in front of you and a batch is brought to your station and you might be sorting incoming mail according to streets or outgoing mail according to town. Here: test me.'

He pulled out a North West Electricity Board pocket diary from his jacket and handed it to me.

'There's maps at the back. Name a town and I'll tell you what county it's in.'

I found the map of England.

'Exeter,' I said.

'Devon,' Ben said. 'Too easy.'

'Milton Keynes.'

'Bucks.'

'Devizes.'

'Wiltshire.'

'Hey, that's pretty impressive. Hartlepool.'

'County Durham.'

'Brilliant.'

'Go on,' he said.

'No,' I said, giving him his diary back. 'You've made your point. If you liked it so much why didn't you stay on?'

'Because it was seasonal. I told you, broth head.'

'What else have you done?'

There was quite a catalogue. He had done more than one labouring job. He had worked in the back room of a chip shop, rumbling spuds and mixing batter. He had worked as a butcher's delivery boy and as an office cleaner. Nothing lasted long. He either walked out or was sacked for poor time keeping or, once, for being drunk.

'Thing is, if you get fired or walk out of a job, you can't claim the dole for six weeks. That, my friend, is a long time to be stony broke. My auntie fed me, and sometimes I even went home now that Sandra was away, till eventually I could sign on. I couldn't get a job, see - not without a decent reference.

'Anyway, you don't get much money on the social and the boredom is incredible. You don't know what to do with yourself. There's no point in getting up in the morning. I got really depressed.

'One day I thought - this is no good. I can't live like this. I went down the Library and scoured the *Telegraph* and the *Blackburn Times*, smartened myself up and landed a job with the 'lectric. And, what do you know, there was my old partner in crime, Stewpot!'

For me these were happy days. The job was easy. Ben and I had plenty of laughs. There was money in our pockets. Our Friday nights were a riot.

I couldn't help thinking, though, that whilst Ben had been going through the rocky period of dead-end jobs and unemployment, I had been thriving in the sixth form. I would soon be going up to Cambridge; clerical work might be Ben's destiny for life.

Most of the time, however, we lived very much in the present, looking forward no further than our Fridays, our pub crawls, and curry or foo yung, or chop suey, or chicken chow mein, savouring our friendship at its peak.

The appeal of these late night diversions at the Ying Kin did not last long. Ben was soon drawn by the lure of the Cavendish Club.

27.   THE CAVENDISH CLUB

THE PRECINCT WAS STATE-OF-THE-ART. The frontage of British Home Stores was ultra-modern plate glass. One fine summer's day, my dad walked straight into one of the doors thinking it was open, and completely lost his sense of humour. We shouldn't have laughed. He had to have a couple of stitches in his nose.

There was a new clock tower. A midget in comparison with the old one, it was faced with brown and white tiles. The oldies dismissed it as a parody. 'It's like a public lavvy turned inside out,' they said. As far as I was concerned, it told the time and that was that.

At the other end of the shopping centre was Lord Square, where there was a ramp up to the shops. In the middle of the square was a fountain which was often made to foam at weekends by jokers who'd bought washing up liquid at Lipton's. Alongside this was the reception area for the Cavendish Club, above which rose a brown-tiled tower. Wrapped around this was a white-tiled staircase. On Friday nights the queue would wind all the way up. A brown-tiled bridge with windows fed from the tower into the night club itself. On the outside, this was a huge white-tiled cube.

Inside, the bouncers checked your tickets and you followed a carpeted corridor, dimly lit with mauve lights, into the club. Incredibly loud music pulsed and crashed into you like a physical thing. There was a circular arena for dancing around which a few steps led up to plush seating areas. A long bar stretched behind the seats, and over to one side was a restaurant which was of no interest to us. What struck you first, apart from the loud pop music with its heavy dance beat, were the spinning kaleidoscopic lights.

It was coming up to closing time for the pubs but still early for the Cavendish. Later, there would be go-go girls and then cabaret. The place attracted some big names from the comedy circuits, including Bob Monkhouse, Dave Allen, Mike Reid and Tommy Cooper.

But Ben wasn't there for the laughs. Ben was there for the girls.

Usually, at this early stage, there would be girls on the dance floor and boys at the bar, sinking lagers, sizing up the talent and summoning up courage to go down there and try to pull. The girls would drop their handbags in a pile in the middle of the floor and dance around them until the first boy was bold enough to come down and join them. The first boy was usually Ben.

I was uncomfortable with the Cavendish. For one thing, I didn't do dancing. For another, the volume of the music meant you couldn't have a conversation.

It's not that I wasn't interested in girls. It wasn't that long since I'd been going out with his sister, after all. I just didn't like this feral hunting and I wasn't comfortable with the idea of one night stands. I'm not being a prude. It just wasn't for me.

What I really didn't like was that until Ben discovered the 'Cav' our Fridays ended as companionably as they started; now they were more likely to end in friction.

The very first time we went there, Ben went to dance, leaving me at the bar. After a while, he came back up, smiling.

'Come on and dance,' he said.

'No, I can't,' I said. 'I don't want to.'

'All right,' he said. 'Let's just go if you're going to be mardy.'

'I'm not being mardy,' I said. 'I was just bored.'

We walked back to our buses in silence.

We didn't go back to the club for two or three weeks. One Friday, we had drunk more than usual. It was one of those balmy evenings you sometimes get in early autumn and the streets were full of young people enjoying themselves. We had drunk quite a lot and were feeling mellow. I yielded to Ben's suggestion.

As usual, we stood at the bar for a while until Ben went down to dance. Shortly afterwards, I saw that he was dancing separately with an attractive blonde girl with back-combed hair, heavy eye make-up, a mini-skirt and long leather boots. Every so often, Ben leaned forward to whisper into her ear. Actually, he was probably bellowing into her ear, given the titanic sound level of the music. Each time, she would throw her head back and laugh.

I was getting very bored. I was frustrated too be-cause there was nobody to blame for my frustration. Ben was doing nothing wrong. I had no claim on him. I didn't feel jealous or anything - just sort of aban-doned - and then I felt embarrassed for feeling like that. I knew I was being ridiculous and that made it worse.

I turned to the bar to order another drink because there was nothing else to do, and, when I turned back, Ben and the girl had disappeared. I scanned the dance floor and the seating areas but they were nowhere to be seen.

I began to feel fed up and increasingly cross, both with Ben and with myself. It was over half an hour before they returned from the direction of the corridor that led to the toilets. You didn't need a degree in behavioural psychology to work out what had been going on.

The girl went down the steps to rejoin her friends. She turned back as she went and gave Ben a little finger wave as he rejoined me at the bar. He lifted a finger to his eyebrow in acknowledgement to her and turned to me.

'Very nice girl that,' he said, grinning smugly. 'Lovely manners. Here, give us a swig of that.'

And he took my lager from me and took a long pull.

'We'd better be going,' he said. 'We'll have missed the last bus and I've got a long walk.'

This was to be our last Friday night together for the time being. A fortnight later I went up to Cambridge.

I was miserable and lonely for quite a while. Other boys from QEGS went up to other colleges that year but they weren't particular friends. Academically, I did all right thanks to the excellent grounding I had at school and thanks to the Joint Play Reading Society [French]. I decided to develop my German as a subsidiary and progressed quickly. The other men in my supervision group (we weren't boys any more, appar-

ently) were all right although there was some snobbery from a couple of public school boys. One of them,
Rupert Carfoys, was particularly obnoxious. His
French was more fluent than mine but much less accurate. Daddy had a little place in the Auvergne, he
said. It later turned out that the 'little place' was a
bloody great castle. He didn't bother me much though
I could have done without his jibes. The evenings felt
long and empty as winter deepened.

I missed Ben, I supposed. There was no point in
writing to him as I knew that there wasn't a hope in
hell of a reply. I don't think he ever bought a postage
stamp in his life. I'd bought some writing paper from
Woolworth's headed with my college's crest. I knew he
wouldn't be impressed but my mum would be.

It was well into the Michaelmas Term before I
made a friend in Cambridge. We were filing out of a
lecture theatre on the Sidgwick Site when a voice at
my shoulder said: 'I liked your question.' I turned to
see a lad with specs and curly hair down to his
shoulders. He was wearing a pea jacket and denim
jeans and looked quite scruffy.

The lecture had been on a set text: *Horace* by
Corneille. My question had been: 'Don't you think
Corneille is a bit over the top. I mean, if you compare
him with Racine. Racine's control of language is tight

and that makes it more powerful, just like forcing water through a narrow channel increases the pressure. Corneille's verse is more like a fractured water main.'

The lecturer had smiled and then there was a pause. He twisted his mouth from side to side. The students began to mutter and I was afraid I'd made a complete dick of myself by trying to show off. Finally, the lecturer spoke.

'I like your analogy,' he said, smiling. 'And there's something in it. On the other hand, I hold it to be a useful maxim never to criticise someone for not doing what he never set out to do in the first place.'

'I liked your analogy too,' the lad went on as we left the building.

'That was one hell of a put down,' I said.

'No, it wasn't,' he said. 'It wasn't unkind at all. He sort of agreed with you and made a proviso, that's all. Do you fancy a coffee?'

I said I did and we made our way to the Buttery. He introduced himself as Adam Klein and said he was a fresher at Corpus. He'd attended an independent school in North London. His family were Jewish and lived in Highgate. They were not particularly orthodox.

I felt rather parochial by comparison though I needn't have worried. Adam and I soon became good friends. We consumed gallons of Nescafe Gold Blend, talking about French literature into the small hours, in his rooms or mine.

He taught me to play squash and his competitiveness reminded me of Ben. Mind you, I was not to be outdone. One night, we played for hours in one of the courts in St Stephen's. I had not yet bought any gear and was playing in bare feet. Eventually my feet were cracked and bleeding but I would not give in. Only when I hit him on the back of his calves with a forearm smash did we call it a day, or rather a night.

'You were not supposed to be there,' I said.

He took it in good part. The next day, he came with me to buy my own racquet, a couple of pairs of shorts and proper squash shoes.

I had not wanted to go into a pub on my own out of shyness, but now that I had a companion we began frequenting The Eagle which Adam said was actually owned by his college. I liked it very much, though the flat and coppery tasting East Anglian beer took some getting used to. I told Adam that I was brought up in a town with three breweries and this was sorry stuff by comparison.

One night, in the lead-up to the end of term, we went to a disco down in the cellars in New Court, St John's - the one that looks like a wedding cake. We were pretty lathered after hours in the pub. It was heaving with people all crushed together and, in the throbbing candy-coloured lights I found myself dancing, as if voluntarily, to *Paint It Black* by the Stones. What's more, I was enjoying it.

The end of term came and I returned to Blackburn. Mum met me at the station, which I hadn't expected, and we went home in a taxi, an unheard of extravagance. At home, the Christmas decorations were up and there was an adorable spaniel puppy which Dad had bought Mum for her birthday. I was treated like the prodigal son. It had never occurred to me that my parents might have missed me. After we'd eaten, Dad took me along to the Whalley Range pub for a 'proper pint' and later I played with the puppy, and all was sweetness and fairy lights.

On the first Friday back, I went up to the North West Electricity Board offices at Whitebirk to see if Ben was still working there. I arrived just before the lunch break and there he was. Everyone was off to the Red Lion and I went along. It was a boozy affair and I have to say I was fêted quite a bit and enjoyed it quite shamelessly. Even the Senior Clerk was there and in a very indulgent mood. Later, when he tried to announce that it was time to go back to the office, he was greeted with a tremendous round of applause and a round of *For he's a jolly good fellow* and then ignored. He left beaming like Scrooge on Christmas morning. After half an hour everyone traipsed back but I doubt if very much work got done that afternoon.

Naturally, Ben and I arranged to meet up in the evening and we did a circular pub crawl in the centre of town. The festive season was brewing and all was jollity and goodwill to all men. Inevitably, Ben suggested we end the evening at the Cavendish, and I didn't put up any objection.

He was gobsmacked when I joined him on his way down to dance, and we stayed on the floor for a few numbers, dancing with this girl and that, or nobody in particular and then, for a laugh, with each other.

He put his arm round my shoulder and said: 'Some crazy moves there, mate. Is that what they teach you in that Cambridge then? Come on. Let's have a drink. You're wearing me out.'

And we went up to the bar. The cold lager was welcome, but I was eager to go down to the dance floor again. They were playing *You really got me* by The Kinks, and I couldn't resist. We went down together again. A mirror ball was throwing flecks of light around like multi-coloured snow. I saw Ben dancing with a girl with long black hair and a pale face, and then he was doing his chat-up routine with his face bent to her ear. Then there were strobe lights and I couldn't see him anywhere.

I went back to the bar and scanned the floor. There was no sign of him or the girl. I thought at first that he must have pulled the same trick as last time and watched the corridor where the toilets were, but half an hour passed, and then the hour, and after an hour and a half I had to face the fact that he'd gone off with the girl without even telling me.

I would only ever see him again once.

In 1972, the Cavendish Club burnt down. The fire was believed to have started in a rubbish chute. It was thought to have been purely accidental.

28.   FLEUR

I WAS MORE THAN HAPPY to return to Cambridge. St Stephen's looked beautiful in a dusting of snow and the loneliness of my first few weeks was a fading memory.

Adam and I studied together, played squash together and drank Guinness in the ingle by the open fire in the Eagle. We dined in each other's halls. We had philosophical arguments about the existence of God, the objective nature of the beautiful and the good, and the meaning of life - as students do - but our disputations were in French, for practice.

When the daffodils blew their yellow trumpets along the Backs, we walked to lectures together through Clare or King's, and began to take ownership of all the beauty around us. This was what I had worked so hard for.

Adam invited me to stay at his home for the first week of the Easter vacation. Theirs was a big Victorian villa filled with books. Every room had bookshelves. The hallway was lined with books and there were little piles of books on the stairs. There were more books in the downstairs lavatory than in our entire house at home.

Adam's parents took to me at once. His father, a small man with wire-framed spectacles, was immensely erudite and spoke six languages. He let me practise my German on him. His mother, an ample woman who wore a cloche hat indoors, really took a shine to me and decided that I needed to be fed whenever possible. I loved the beautifully braided challah bread that appeared at breakfast, crispy and golden on the outside and fluffy on the inside. There was matzoh ball soup and delicious brisket with apricots, cooked all day so that it melted in your mouth. My favourite had to be potato latkes, deep fried in oil, although Mrs Klein's apple cake was also sublime.

Adam showed me London. We went to the National Gallery and saw *The Barber of Seville* at The Coliseum and *Elektra* at the Round House in Chalk Farm. It was in the original Greek but it was incredibly powerful all the same. I was fascinated by the Tube and the smoky wind that blew around the stations. The river left me awestruck as did Westminster Abbey, and the Houses of Parliament.

Mrs Klein invited me to stay on, but I knew my parents would be hurt if I didn't go home, though to be honest, I was beginning to feel metropolitan and Blackburn was beginning to seem like a backwater, rather than the centre of the universe it had been for me as a child. This time I made no attempt to contact Ben.

Back in Cambridge, the willows by the Cam had shivered down their green, and Adam and I learned to punt - the hard way. Trial and error taught us that the best way to get under Silver Street Bridge was to aim away from it and let the current swing you round; that you were less likely to fall off the platform if you took your shoes and socks off, and that if the pole got stuck in the mud, you gave it a twist. Once, a miscalculation meant that my pole went smack against King's College Bridge. The punt and Adam sailed blithely on while I clung to the pole and slithered slowly down into the water. Adam fell in once as a result of being attacked by an angry swan. Actually, it did no more than flap its wings at him and lower its neck, but he swore it was out to kill him.

In my second year, I acquired a girlfriend from New Hall. Lucinda was rather upper crust and had a double-barrelled name which I can no longer remember. She was a ferocious feminist and relieved me of certain chauvinist prejudices which I hadn't been aware of, along with my virginity, of which I had been very much aware for a long time. She was reading English and did French as a subsidiary. She wasn't very good at it, and I used to help her out with her translations, which seemed a good trade off for my sexual initiation.

I wasn't in love or anything and neither was she, but we were very comfortable with each other. Adam said he thought Lucinda was gorgeous and added, rather ruefully, that: 'Orthodox or unorthodox, Mama Klein will want me to marry a nice Jewish girl. Papa Klein not so much, but Mama Klein wears the trousers at Château Klein.'

All the same he found himself a Lithuanian girl from one of the language schools on Station Road.

'What Mama Klein doesn't know won't hurt her,' he said happily.

We went out as a foursome, to the pub, to the Arts Cinema, to the Varsity Restaurant. I was beginning to feel very grown up. At the beginning of the Easter Term, Lucinda threw me over for an unfeasibly thin creep who wore drainpipe trousers in electric crimson or lime green and Byronic shirts with puffed sleeves. His jet black hair came down to his bum. The attraction for her was that he was the lead singer in a rock band called *Coccyx*. I mean how pretentious can you get? His stage name was Rupert Clavier, for God's sake. Anyway, she was besotted and I was desolate.

My desolation lasted a week or so. It had its upside. I began to work ferociously hard and at the end of term I took a first in Part I. Adam was awarded a 2:1 and he and the Kleins were very happy with that.

In your third year in the Modern and Medieval Languages Faculty at Cambridge you have the option of taking a year abroad, returning to Cambridge for your finals year. I had been looking forward to this keenly but also with some trepidation. Adam found it hard to believe that I had never been abroad before.

Anyway, I managed to find myself a placement as an English assistant at a school in Tours and Adam was offered an internship in a bank in Lyon. We promised each other that we'd keep in touch but that didn't quite work out.

I was enchanted by Tours from the outset. With the MML faculty's help, I rented a small apartment in le Vieux Tours - the old town. It was small and very basic but it had two huge windows that stretched from floor to ceiling, and each of them had a little balcony from which I could watch the comings and goings in the narrow cobbled street below. A wisteria vine climbed around the outside of these windows and, when I first arrived at my new home in early summer, the clusters of purple flowers were in extravagant bloom. There was a little kitchen curtained off in a corner, an ornate desk, a very high double bed, and an ivory-coloured rococo wardrobe so enormous that it was hard to imagine how it ever got up to this fourth floor level.

The stairs were narrow and draughty. They were lit by naked bulbs operated by a timer switch but the illumination didn't last quite long enough between floors. I got used to finding the keyhole by touch alone.

The shared shower was in a narrow alcove on the staircase and the lock was broken so that I lived in fear of being caught naked by the old woman on the floor below. Thankfully, it never happened. The lavatory was in another alcove halfway up the stairs to the garret where there lived a middle-aged man with a very obvious toupé and a walrus moustache. Fortunately, the loo had a functioning lock.

These were the unfortunate disadvantages, but my pleasure in having a place of my own for the first time in my life far outweighed the inconveniences. And the *quartier* was so romantic and charming that I couldn't help relishing my independence.

I had been lucky in my placement too. The school lay in the lee of the cathedral. There was a high wall in the playground beyond which arose the flying buttresses of *la Cathédrale Saint-Gatien,* and this made me feel rather privileged to be there.

The staff made me very welcome and I found the kids delightful: bright, curious and engaging. Of course I was not much older than the students in the *première* and *terminale* classes, the equivalent of our sixth form, and I probably learnt more from them than they did from me.

There were things that took some getting used to. For one thing, the school day started earlier and finished earlier. I was surprised that three courses were served at lunchtime and that staff could have a glass of wine. There were pigeon-holes in the staffroom where your napkin was kept, and you took it into the refectory with you.

Back then, everybody smoked - I was something of an exception. During morning break, I was amazed to see the students smoking in the playgrounds, even the younger kids. There was no uniform and the students' casual clothes struck me as very colourful. Oddly enough, when I showed a middle school class a form photograph from my second year at QEGS, the French kids declared that they would love to have a school uniform with royal blue blazers.

I suddenly remembered being told that when he left school, two years before I did, Ben hung his blazer from a tree in Corporation Park, doused it in lighter fuel, and set fire to it. But that was in another universe, or so it seemed, and long, long ago.

My departmental colleagues were very sociable and gathered roughly once a week for dinner at one of the excellent restaurants on the Rue Colbert. We would often meet beforehand for an *apéro* at *Le Musée,* a lively café on the Rue Nationale, and it was in *Le Musée* that I met my wife, Fleur.

29.   AN ORDINARY LIFE

THAT WAS OVER FORTY YEARS AGO and I have not for a single moment had cause to regret it. I thought Fleur was stunning from the very first moment she walked in with Jacqueline, a colleague in the department. They had been friends since their schooldays and they are still in touch even after all this time. I have always harboured a suspicion that Jacqueline was involved in a little matchmaking but, believe me, I am not complaining.

Fleur has emerald eyes and copper-coloured hair, cut in a bob with a severe fringe. She has the Frenchwoman's capacity to look elegant whatever she's doing. Her clothes were not necessarily expensive back then but they looked it. To me she was chic, even when she had just got out of bed, padding barefoot round my apartment in my threadbare bathrobe. In fact, she looked particularly fetching with the robe slipping off her freckled shoulder as she made our breakfast coffee.

We were friends and then lovers in no time. Fleur saw to that. My floral sweetheart has always had a no-

nonsense attitude which English friends sometimes find a little brusque on first meeting. She is always totally forthright, doesn't mince her words, and sees no point in wasting time or emotional energy on nuance or reserve. I have to say that in this respect she has been very good for me: she is an excellent antidote to my tendency to dither and faff about. And if friends found her a little abrupt, even tart, at first, she would soon win them over with her charm, and genuine kindness.

At weekends, we visited the châteaux of the Loire, and I was blown away by their beauty and splendour. Chenonceau particularly, with its arched bridge over the Cher, captivated me. We had a weekend trip to Paris, where we met up with Adam, and got very drunk in the Latin quarter. Thanks to Fleur and my students, my French was improving massively.

During the Easter holiday of my year in France, Fleur and I visited Cambridge and Blackburn. I was not surprised that she was enchanted by the architectural fantasia that is Cambridge - and my college in particular - but I was astonished that she liked Blackburn so much. She said she liked the civic pride in the public buildings. She thought the place was 'authentic' and had all the honest virtues of a provincial town and none of the airs and graces of a city. I thought this indicated a very French mind set but said nothing.

She got on well with my mother.

'She speaks as she finds,' Mum said, 'and I like that in a woman.'

My father treated her with a kind of shy and exaggerated formality which I thought was a bit absurd, but Fleur was charmed.

She loved the markets and developed a taste for Kenyon's pies. She raved about black pudding and loved the tripe stall in the food hall. I could never abide the stuff but she said the stall was the equal to any *triperie* in France.

She loved the green double-decker buses and applauded them whenever they passed us in the street, with the heels of her hands together like a child.

Best of all she liked Corporation Park. We had seen plenty of French formal gardens in our tours of the châteaux of the Loire valley. She said they were all very well, but claimed that the eye soon tired of the symmetries.

'But, don't you see, Stuart? This is so much better. Every time you go round a bend there is a different view, and it also changes because we are going up a slope.'

I was pleased because so much of my childhood had been played out in this place and I liked sharing it with her. After all, this had been my daily route to school, with Ben and later, Tom. It was part of my identity. The slope led up to the two lakes with their ducks and geese and swans. She loved the conservatory (now vandalised and boarded up). There were exotic plants I couldn't name. They grew in a green light and the air was cool and moist. Our feet clanged on the grating underfoot. Outside, finches and budgerigars chattered and quarrelled in their aviary.

A number of graded terraces led up to the Broad Walk. Then deeply wooded paths wound up the steep incline to the Cannons and Revidge. This was the area Fleur liked best because it was so 'un-French'. From up here, we could see a panorama of factory chimneys and church spires and towers, though the Industrial Revolution had long been over for Blackburn, and the churches were emptying, as the young began to turn their backs on whatever seemed associated with authority.

I told her that, once upon a time, there was a colossal chimney on Bennington Street, known as the Great Destructor, which belched out the smoke from the town's waste incinerators. By comparison with this monster, all the chimneys she could see were no more than pea-shooters. I showed her the narrow tower of St Philip's and the decorated tower of St Silas's. Down below, the soot-blackened shape of Holy Trinity, where Ben and I had been scouts once upon a time, stood on its mount, surrounded by the wastes of slum clearance. And we could see the cupola of St John's, where we had been choristers long, long ago, and looked and sang like angels, but sometimes behaved like the devil's own imps.

I told Fleur about the time Ben put a firework up his bum. She was unimpressed and unamused.

'He sounds like an idiot,' she said.

Soon it was time for Fleur to go back to Tours and for me to return to Cambridge for my finals year. We saw each other as often as we could, in England or in France, though money was quite tight. It was often enough, however, for me to be quite sure that I wanted to spend the rest of my life with her. I proposed to her on Clare Bridge in the February of that year as we looked down over the frozen river, and she accepted straight away. We married at Cambridge Registry Office on the same day as my graduation. The reception was at the Red Lion in Grantchester and there was another, much more lavish, a fortnight later at *Les Jets d'Eau* in Tours, organised and paid for by Fleur's parents.

I know I'm going on and on about me, when I've already said that this is really Ben's story, not mine. Bear with me a little longer. Ben is about to make his final appearance.

I know that many people, on graduating, drift into teaching in a daze, especially if they've read an arts subject. Perhaps the risks and rigours of journalism don't suit; perhaps life as an advertising copywriter seems too pressured and shallow; perhaps transferring your skills to a desk job in the Civil Service seems secure but soulless. Perhaps such people are looking for a more ordinary life? An easier life, even?

Well, I was lucky in a way because I really wanted to teach. I wanted to 'make a difference' as the cliché has it, and my brief stint at the school in Tours had been fun and seemed to confirm my vocation. I had to decide whether I wanted to teach English in France or French in England. Fleur, by now a confirmed anglophile, decided the conundrum for us, and I was soon persuaded that she was right, and that I was more likely to flourish in the English independent system than in the state-regulated French régime, where we could be required to move school at the whim of some bureaucrat in Paris.

For some time, Fleur had been working as a translator and received assignments from various agencies.

She could translate to and from French and English, was totally reliable and returned copy swiftly, so she was in much demand. Much of the work was technical stuff and it was, according to Fleur, *aussi ennuyeux qu'une poignée de haricots* (as boring as a handful of beans) which I took to mean *very* boring. On the other hand, it could be lucrative work, depending on the commissioning company, and there were months, especially at first, when she brought home more than I did.

My first post was at a grammar school which in atmosphere and academic stature was much like QEGS. It was situated amongst sand dunes on a windy stretch of coast, and my classroom (Number 7) looked out to sea.

Any illusion that it might be an easy life was dispelled in my very first lesson. I was baptised in fire and brimstone. My pupils swapped desks every time I turned to the blackboard; the air was thick with paper aeroplanes, and some of the boys were actually coming and going through the open windows.

At break that morning, the colleague who had the classroom next to mine came over to me, removing the milky skin from his coffee with a spoon. He was small and whiskery and resembled a benign beaver. He seemed to me to be very old. Patches of his academic gown were green and shiny. I learned later that the boys loved and revered him.

'Giving you a rough time of it, are they?' he said.

'I'm afraid they are,' I said.

'Hmm, they've always been a rowdy lot,' he said. 'Of course, your predecessor's dramatic exit hasn't helped.'

'How do you mean?'

'Oh dear,' he said, 'weren't you told? That's very remiss of the Head, you know. You should have been told.'

'Why? What happened?'

'Well, you see, their tutor, Mr Sprague, was a hopeless drunk. He would come into school obviously inebriated. Heaven knows how he got away with it. There were rumours that he had something on the Head and was blackmailing him; others said that he was very rich and had promised to make the school a very healthy endowment in the future. Well, I couldn't say, you know.

'He made no attempt to teach the boys anything. He used to set them work and then sit at his desk reading *The Daily Telegraph*. Well, of course, the boys weren't having this and went berserk.

'One day, old Sprague had had enough. He was particularly sodden that afternoon and the boys were more than usually feral. One of them broke a window with a cricket ball and the others had begun chanting.

'Sprague stood up, folded the *Telegraph* neatly, placed it in the centre of the desk and left the classroom. He walked down the corridor, through the entrance hall, out to his car. Then he shot down the drive at about sixty, lost control and drove up a sand dune, overturning the car. Killed immediately, poor old sod.'

'Dear God,' I said.

'Dear God, indeed. It was a shock to us all, as you can imagine. I expect the boys have concluded that, having seen off one master, they might as well start work on you.'

'Dear God,' I said.

'You keep saying that,' he said. 'Well, I'll let you get on.'

He turned to replenish his coffee and then turned back.

'Let me give you a little tip,' he said. 'Do not under any circumstances attempt to entertain them; never tell jokes; do make it clear to them that you consider them to be a distinct and intellectually inferior species; make sure they understand that, in the last analysis, you hold all the cards; avoid overusing sanctions

- they quickly become devalued and the boys can tell that you are hiding behind them.

'When you have tamed them, you may relent a little. You might allow yourself the occasional smile. Gradually, you will build a rapport with them. It usually takes a term.'

And he turned away to talk to colleagues about cricket.

I have to say that the rest of the day was much better. The sixth formers were bright and happy to be taught by someone not much older than them, the younger kids were biddable, and my fourth form were precocious boys who were funny and a bit wild, but keen to learn. It took time with the Remove. I followed the Beaver's advice, in spirit, though not to the letter, and gradually we were able to work together and have some fun on the way. It helped when they discovered that I had a beautiful French wife.

I was just thirty when I accepted a post at an independent school in the south London suburbs. Fleur wasn't sure she wanted to move to the capital, but she didn't want to stand in the way of my career, and she said she could do her own work anywhere where it was quiet. She soon got used to metropolitan life and made friends of her own. She would certainly have let me know if she were uneasy.

The terms came and went, with fresh, clean-smelling stationery at Michaelmas, the drudgery of mock exams in Lent, Speech Day and cricket and strawberry teas in Summer. We spent the long vacations in France and we were very happy.

It wasn't perfect. We had our quarrels, as all couples do. They were pretty cataclysmic, with Fleur ranting at me in French and me trying to calm her down in English. She threw things too and - unhappily for me - she was a very good shot. However, these rows were short. It would be like the drama of a summer storm: trees thrashing about then suddenly still; sky goes black; rain pelts down; thunder and lightning - then, just as suddenly, the storm passes and the wet garden smells fresh and sweet. I sometimes think these rows kept us together. They were usually about nothing much and there were never any repercussions.

Sometimes, after a row, Fleur would say: 'I enjoyed that.'

The one serious blow to our contentment was that we couldn't have children. After trying for two years we consulted doctors and went through any number of tests, but they could not identify any particular cause of infertility in either of us. It seems that this is not at all uncommon. Gradually, we became used to the situation. At least we had each other and there was no cause for any kind of subliminal blame game. Sometimes, no doubt, we felt a twinge of disappointment in the company of friends with cute kids, though there was a perverse sort of consolation when we saw them trapped at home amid steaming nappies and screaming offspring.

It was in our third year in London that my mother rang me up with some grim news.

Ben was in prison for arson.

30.   PRISON

THE PRISON WAS SITUATED on the outskirts of a charac-terless town in the West Midlands. I won't name it. It would seem unfair to Ben for reasons I can't quite identify. I caught a mid-morning train from Euston, changing to a one-carriage cattle truck at Birming-ham, completing the last leg by bus. As we approached I could see from the top deck that the perimeter wall was formidable. Not only was it high and featureless but a vast concrete cylinder ran along the top, so that anyone attempting to get in or out would somehow have to climb up the underside of a curve.

There was a red brick gatehouse with castellations and a massive wooden gate, painted a reddish brown, into which was set a very small door, which would let just one person pass through at a time. The gate seemed like a grim parody of the gatehouses of certain Cambridge colleges. By the gate was a newly-painted white flagpole from which the union jack hung limply, on this stifling July afternoon. Close by was a red pil-lar box on which the letters VR were inscribed.

The prison was directly opposite a hospital and I couldn't help thinking that the good people of this dull little town had parked their embarrassing undesirables out on the periphery: the lawless, the dangerous, the sick, the old. Out of sight, out of mind.

Just by the bus stop was a prefab office - the Visitor Centre - and there was already a queue building up outside. Many of these people seemed to know each other and the mood was surprisingly upbeat. There were several young girls with baby buggies, some with toddlers in tow; there were elderly couples and single women, but I think I was the only young adult male. Bang on the appointed time we were let in.

First we were led into a locker room where we were allocated a locker. We had to deposit everything about our persons in there, right down to hankies. Absolutely nothing was allowed beyond this point apart from the locker key, the printed pass and a few coins for the vending machines.

From here we were shepherded into a waiting room. I was surprised by the atmosphere of fellow feeling in here. Wives, mothers, fathers, girlfriends, children - all in the same boat, all here to try to bring some cheer to souls upon whom society was taking its revenge, justly or not. The prison staff were really friendly too, and I had an inkling that visiting time was, for them, a bright moment in an otherwise grim day.

I don't remember everything in too much detail. It was some time ago now. We queued to go through security. I recall a corridor with dogs. Everywhere the windows were above head height so that there was plenty of light but no views. The procedure was rather like airport security. We passed through a metal detector arch and were then searched very thoroughly. Finally, we were finger-printed, which I hadn't expected and which I found faintly comical, although I could see the point. It wasn't to prevent us nicking something from the nick, as it were. I thought it might be to help trace the provenance of any illicit package that might somehow have got through security, though God knows how. After the visit, the reason became clear. We were fingerprinted on the way out too. It was to prevent prisoners escaping.

Then there was another waiting room. We were to be admitted all at once so we had to wait until everyone had gone through security.

This gave me time to notice that pretty well all the others were a bit scruffy. I don't want to be snobbish or anything; I was just made vividly aware of the enduring relationship between crime and poverty. Perhaps the wealthy are paragons of virtue, or maybe they can afford more expensive lawyers, or maybe they're just better at not getting caught.

At last, we all filtered into a long room, with institutionalised pea-green paint halfway up the walls, and institutionalised grey above. The room was bright: the sunshine outside came through skylights and long thin windows high up, almost at the level of the roof.

The prisoners were all seated at low coffee tables, one to each table, with their backs to the wall and dressed in orange high-viz vests. Otherwise they wore ordinary casual clothes. A maximum of three visitors was allowed for each prisoner. I expected a heavy presence of warders with keys on a great metal ring or on chains but, in fact, they kept a low profile.

I caught sight of Ben's blond hair at the far end of the long room and went towards him. He was pulling one of his trademark faces expressing mock surprise, although he'd known I was coming.

I passed a couple of men whose faces looked desolate as it became clear to them that their visitors weren't going to turn up. Ben stood to shake hands with me. We had only gone in for hugging when we were toddlers or when we were drunk.

'You haven't changed,' I said. It was true. His hair was shorter but he still retained his boyish looks.

'Really?' he said. 'I don't think orange suits me. You've changed terribly.'

'How do you mean?'

'You look really old.'

'Do I? That'll be the teaching.'

'Is that what you do?' he said. 'Yeah, I can imagine that.'

'Actually, being amongst kids has a kind of rejuvenating effect. Mind you, Old Father Time begins to get to you in the end. How long has it been?'

'I dunno. You tell me.'

'I reckon it must be about twelve years.'

'About that, yeah.'

'So what's the secret of eternal youth?'

'Being banged up twenty-three hours a day? Prison food? Intellectual company? I couldn't say.'

'Yeah, sorry,' I said. 'Listen, would you like a coffee?'

'I would, yes,' he said. 'Thanks.'

And he smiled for the first time since my arrival.

I came back with coffee and several Twix and Mars Bars. The coffee was surprisingly good. Ben was quiet for a while. This was obviously something of a treat for him.

'I didn't know whether to get you fags,' I said.

'I'm in here for arson, pal. Do you think they'd let me have the means to light a fag? Anyway, I've given up.'

'Sorry. I didn't think.'

'No, you didn't.'

There was a pause. Ben opened a Twix and offered me one of the bars. I shook my head.

'So what's it like then?' I asked. I could tell that Ben was not going to initiate any part of the conversation and I was a little embarrassed. After all, I'd never been in this position before and I didn't want to be tactless.

'Oh, pretty much as you'd expect. Full English breakfast in bed at ten. Read the papers in the Library at eleven. Campari and soda at noon and a running buffet luncheon at one. A stroll around the grounds in the afternoon and cards after dinner.

'What the hell do you think it's like? It's like *Porridge* only smellier and noisier and dirtier and more dangerous and a million times more boring.'

'Sorry,' was all I could manage to say.

'No, I'm sorry,' Ben said. 'That wasn't fair.'

"It's OK,' I said.

'It's the boredom that gets to you,' Ben continued. 'If they're short-staffed, which is often, you're locked in your cell for hours on end with nothing to do. I can read for a bit but if we haven't been allowed in the Library for a few days, that's it. Besides, I've read pretty well all they've got that's of any interest.

'I tried reading the Bible once. A lot of it was familiar from choir obviously, but the Old Testament - well, it starts all right, but then, after a while - well, you know the kind of novel that has too many names and you leave off for a bit and when you come back, you've no idea what's going on? It's like that.

'Anyway, you get a numb arse from reading for too long.

'Worst of all is Lobotomy.'

'Come again.'

'My cell mate,' Ben said. 'He's really called Ronny Lobb but we call him 'Lobotomy' because parts of his brain are missing. You'd get better conversation from a nematode worm, which is a laugh because he never stops talking.'

'What's he in for?' I asked.

'It's strange,' Ben said. 'Nobody asks that question very much in here. It's as if all crimes are equal and we are all doing time and that's that. Apart from the nonces and rapists, that is. They are in a separate wing and have exercise at a different time - for their own protection. Not many people know what I'm in for but

I get the feeling that for those who do, arson commands a certain respect.

'Everybody knows what Lobotomy is in for because he never stops telling people. Lobotomy is the world's worst burglar. As soon as he's out of here, he will pull another job and ten-to-one he'll get caught. The screws think he's a joke and the courts despair of him. He doesn't mind though. In here he gets three meals a day and a roof over his head. There's nothing for him out there.'

'What's the food like?' I asked. 'And don't say caviar and lobster.'

'It's bland and repetitive,' Ben said. 'But what you really mean is: do they spit into the soup in the kitchens and put bogies in the mashed potatoes?'

'Sort of,' I said.

'Well, I wouldn't be able to tell, would I?' Ben said. 'I think they reserve that sort of stuff for the kiddie fiddlers.'

'Do you get on all right with the other prisoners?'

'When we're let out for association, yeah, for the most part,' Ben said. 'It was really hard at first, I have to admit. The bullying can be pretty brutal and newbies are put through it a bit. I let it be known that I could handle myself early on. I told Lobotomy to tell people I was handy with a razor. Truth is, I wouldn't stand a chance if it came to a rumble, but everything is about bluff in here. I just try to keep a low profile. I keep my nose clean with the screws because I want time off for good behaviour, but I take good care not to be seen brown-nosing. And apart from that I keep myself to myself as much as possible.

'It doesn't help to have a pretty face in here, though. I was advised early on not to drop the soap in the showers.'

'Sorry?' I said.

'Bit slow, aren't you?' Ben said. 'There are no women in here. I don't want to get browned, do I? If you drop your hat, you kick it home, as they say.'

I got the point and wished I hadn't. I thought I'd better change the subject.

'What I don't get,' I said, 'is why you did it, Ben.'

'Why I set the fires, you mean?'

'Yeah.'

'It was the voices, wasn't it? I heard voices telling me to do it.'

31. THE FIRE ON TONTINE STREET

I KNEW FROM WHAT MY MOTHER HAD SAID on the phone and from a subsequent check of the papers in Blackburn Library that Ben had been found guilty of setting fire to a warehouse near Ainsworth Street. It was about to close down because the building had been condemned as a result of slum clearance, and most of the contents had already been removed. Nobody had been hurt in the incident, though Ben had used an accelerant in starting the fire. That was not good news because it was evidence of intent. He had been sentenced to custody of one year and four months.

Fleur and I were in Blackburn for my father's funeral. A few days after Mum had phoned me about Ben, she rang again to say that my father had had a massive heart attack in Lloyd's bank. We rushed north and were in time to be with him when he died quietly in the Infirmary. The service and cremation were at Pleasington.

During this time I felt a great unease, laced with guilt. I felt guilty that I hardly knew my father. He had been a kind but elusive presence during my childhood.

Could I have tried harder to get close to him? I felt guilty about Ben too. Had it been an overreaction to let our friendship lapse? He had gone off with a girl and left me stranded in a night club. So what? Was it such a big deal? Did I expect him to report to me whenever he pulled? Wasn't it out of all proportion?

I put all this to Fleur as we drove back to London. She was dismissive.

'And do you think that, if you had remained friends, Ben would have stayed on the straight and narrow? You think you have that much power over him? Pffft. He is a bad egg. Forget about him.'

'You don't understand,' I said.

'I understand perfectly. You have a fixation. You can't see that the Ben who was your best chum when you were little boys is not the same as the man who sets fire to things.'

'You really don't understand,' I said.

'As you wish,' Fleur said, 'but spare me your sentimentality. And another thing. Do you really think anything you could have done or said over the years would have prevented your father from being stricken down in the bank when his time came?'

I could see that a row was brewing so I just said, 'probably not,' and let it drop.

Back in London, I brooded for a couple of days and decided that I was going to visit Ben despite Fleur's disapproval. I wrote to him asking if he'd like a visit; he replied and said that he would. Formal applications were set in train and my visitor's permit arrived in the post.

Now here I was listening to my friend telling me that he'd been led on by Satanic voices.

'What exactly did they say?' I asked.

He put on a Halloween voice.

'"Ben," they said. "Ben. Burn things. Burn things, Ben. Burn *everything*!"'

'You're pulling my leg, aren't you?' I said.

'Of course I'm pulling your leg, you soft get. Come on. Demonic voices? I ask you!'

I laughed.

'There is a supernatural element to all this, though,' I said. 'Do you remember that choir trip to Blackpool? When you had your fortune told by that gypsy woman. I can't remember her name.'

'Yeah,' he said, grinning, 'it was a good day that, wasn't it? She said my world would be turned upside down, and then there was that upside-down house on the Pleasure Beach. Proper did my head in, that did.'

'Do you remember what else she said?'

'No. What did she say?'

'She said that one day you'd set the world on fire,' I said.

'Bollocks,' Ben said. 'You made that up, just to freak me out.'

'I did not,' I said. 'That is exactly what you told me she'd said when you came out of the booth.'

'Bloody hell, that's creepy,' Ben said.

'Who's the soft get now?' I said. 'It's all formulaic, like horoscopes. She'd have a repertoire of prophecies and she'd dish them out at random, one good, one bad. And they'd all be ambiguous so that there could never be any comeback if some idiot lost his life savings on the gee-gees or rogered his best friend's wife.'

'Cynical bugger, aren't you?' Ben said.

I ignored him.

'You still haven't told me why you did it,' I said.

'What is this?' Ben said. 'Are you suddenly my shrink or summat? I get enough of this in therapy, you know.'

'And what do you tell them?'

'What they expect to hear, of course, the nosy bastards,' Ben said with a grin. 'With a good deal of fancy embroidery sometimes. They love it. They scribble away and write me up in learned papers which are read in all the best universities, probably even yours, me old cock sparrow.'

I did not rise to this jibe.

'How about telling *me* the truth, though?' I said. 'For old times' sake.'

Ben gave me a look of faint distaste and then seemed to recede into himself. He was looking at nothing in particular.

'It's the flames, how they move and change shape, sometimes smooth, sometimes jagged, and the colours: yellow, orange and blue, but sometimes a flash of green or purple. And the rushes of sparks. And the noise: roaring, crackling, hissing, spitting and whistling. And the crash of collapsing timbers and the brightness of melting lead. And the smell of the smoke.'

He came out of his trance and looked at me directly.

'I get off on it, Stuart,' he said.

I shifted in my chair.

'Oh, not sexually,' he said. 'You can wipe that puritanical leer off your face. It's better than sex. It's a different dimension.'

'How did they catch you?' I said. I'd been wanting to ask this for a while and, since things were turning candid, I thought I could ask it now.

'Ah, my stupidity, Stewpot,' Ben said. 'Pure stupidity. You see, once I've set a fire, I have to go back and see how it's going. On this occasion I'd been seen going into the building. Curse this blond hair. I should have worn some sort of hat. What do you think? A beret? A fedora? Anyway, when I'd splashed some petrol about on some bales of stuff, I slipped out again and went away. I think I went into St John's Tavern and had a pint while I waited.

'When I heard the fire engines I went back to the scene. I always do. You get this incredible sense of power.'

'Always?' I blurted out. 'You mean there have been other fires?'

Ben covered his face with both hands and spoke through his fingers.

'Shush, you idiot,' he whispered. 'Walls have ears, especially these walls.'

'Sorry,' I said, not entirely sure why, or even if I was.

'There was quite a crowd there,' Ben continued, 'and I was identified. The woman who'd seen me going in, from behind her net curtains, had also seen me coming out. She recognised me in the crowd and tipped off the police who were there with the firemen. I was taken in as a suspect there and then. Later on, forensics found my fingerprints on the petrol can that

I'd just thrown aside. You wouldn't think fingerprints would survive a fire, would you?'

'I can't say I've ever given it much thought but no, I suppose not.' I dropped my voice to a whisper. 'Are you serious? There've been other fires? Or are you pulling my leg again?'

'Do you remember when we followed the fire engines along Randall Street?'

'Very vaguely.'

'We were walking home from school and you said you wanted to go into the sweet shop at the junction. I said I thought I must have dropped my maths book and that I'd have to go back and look for it.'

'I'm surprised you even cared,' I said.

'I didn't,' he replied. 'I hadn't dropped it at all. Anyway, when I got back to you, three fire engines came past and headed up Randall Street back the way we'd come. I said: "come on let's see" and we ran after them to where there was a fire in an empty depot on the corner of Tontine Street.'

'I remember now,' I said.

'It was glorious,' Ben said. 'There were five hose-pipes trained on the building at one point. It was nearly dark and it was just a black silhouette against a red sky with flames spewing out of the windows. It was amazing because no-one bothered about us, nobody shooed us away. We got quite close up while the crowd hung back.'

'Why are you telling me this, Ben?' I said, suddenly guessing the answer.

'Because, it was me. I did it. It was my fire.'

There was a pause. I was very shocked.

'I don't want to hear any more of this stuff, Ben,' I said. 'You put me in a very compromising position.'

'You're not going to grass on me, are you?'

'No, I'm not,' I said, knowing that I should, 'but the less I know the better. Let's change the subject.'

'Suit yourself,' Ben said, opening another Twix bar.

'Did you stay on at the Electricity Board?' I asked.

'Nah. It was all right at first,' Ben said. 'And for a while afterwards but it wasn't going anywhere. You know, when we got our first pay packets, it were like we were millionaires. But you get to looking around you and you see what other people are earning and you realise you're on peanuts. One Friday afternoon, after I'd checked the papers, I took a look at the pay grades. Thing is, you move up the ladder so slowly. Fred Vole, who'd been there 35 years and was on the top intermediate grade, was still earning peanuts. Even the Senior Clerk was earning less than many a skilled manual worker.'

'So you got out?'

'So I got out.'

'What did you do?'

'A bit of this and a bit of that. I get bored easily, you see. The best one was when I got a motorbike and set up my own courier business. I enjoyed that. I was doing quite well for a couple of years but the recession kicked in and my clients began to say that they couldn't afford to fast track their packages and would have to go back to using the Royal Mail for everything instead. Besides, the bike started playing up and I had next to no capital because I'd been spending as fast as I'd been earning.

'It was a bad time. Mum was showing signs of confusion and forgetting things and it was getting worse. She'd forget to eat or have her tea and then start making tea again as soon as she'd washed up. The doctors said it was early onset dementia. I left my auntie's and went home to look after her. My Auntie Helen was on the point of throwing me out anyway. Said I was too old to be sponging off her.

'It was hopeless and in the end Mum had to go into a home. I visited her once a week, but after a few months she didn't recognise me so I went less often. I can't go now, obviously.

'Anyway, this is boring. What have you been up to?'

I told him about my time in France and I told him all about Fleur.

'Lucky you,' he said. 'She sounds cool. I didn't think you had it in you.'

'Yeah, sometimes I don't believe my luck,' I said. 'I often think I don't deserve her. Even after all this time.'

'You probably don't,' Ben said.

I ignored this, and told him about my teaching career, starting with my baptism of fire and the paper aeroplanes and the boys rioting under my nose.

Ben laughed.

'I wish I'd been in your class,' he said.

'I'm glad you weren't,' I said.

I told him about the move to London and how my career had developed there. Ben seemed to be getting distracted and fidgety.

'Any kids?' he said.

'No,' I said. 'We can't.'

'Low sperm count?' he said with a big grin on his face.

'No, the doctors couldn't find anything wrong with either of us.'

'Except you can't have kids?'

'Except we can't have kids.'

'It's ironic, isn't it?' Ben said. 'You can't have kids and I only have to look at a girl and she's pregnant.'

I thought it was time to change the subject.

'Do you ever hear from your dad?' I said. 'Does he visit?'

'No,' Ben said. 'I'd punch his lights out if I saw him again.'

'Sandra?'

'That stuck-up cow? No. I don't think she even knows I'm in here.'

Prison officers were moving up and down the rows, telling guests and inmates that the one and a half hours were nearly up. There was a general sense of movement, a packing of bags and a scraping of chairs. I wondered if Ben had any other visitors at all.

'Would you like me to come again?' I said.

'I don't think so,' he replied, head down.

'It's no trouble,' I said. 'Well, not much, now I know the ropes. It's the school holidays and everything.'

'Don't bother,' he said, looking at me.

'Why not? I really don't mind.'

'Because you're boring, Stuart,' Ben said. 'You always were.'

32.   TOM

NOW THAT I'M RETIRED, I often meet up with Tom Catlow, the friend from my schooldays who gained a brief spell of fame when he and a mutual friend called Will Melling solved the century-old conundrum of 'the skelly in the bog'. You may have read about it. It was in the papers.

My own career had been unspectacular but rewarding, and I like to think I may have done some good in the world in my modest fashion. I'd worked my way up to the position of Second Master at my school in London. I was in the classroom less and less and in my office more and more, as the profession became more and more strangled in red tape, meaningless data-gathering, gimmicky initiatives, and other Byzantine manifestations of bureaucracy. When the opportunity arose to give all this up, I took it. I would miss the children but, so be it.

There is not much to be said for ageing. It creeps up on you. Your mirror reminds you that you are not Dorian Gray. The lines around your eyes and mouth are slight at first, and you look twice in case it's a trick of the light. But it isn't. You become accustomed bit by bit to these disfigurements - Time is kind only in that his etchings on your face are very gradual. But then you notice that one eyelid is drooping ever so slightly compared to the other, that you are developing jowls, that there are hairs inside and outside your ears. If you crouch to pick up something from the floor, you are not entirely sure that you will ever be able to stand up again. You spend more time with the dentist and Specsavers.

And yet, on a good day, you feel just as lively in spirit as when you were much younger. I am still the kid who sang in the choir, who won the Wide Game in the scouts, who trespassed in the waxworks, the same kid who ran the Joint Play Reading Society [French] along with Sandra Westwell. And I look in the mirror again and think that there is some strange trickery going on. This is not my body. I am the victim of some cosmic joke.

Fleur is ageing too, of course, though I am with her every day and the process is so infinitesimal that you hardly notice. Besides, she is French and so perfectly groomed that her beauty seems invulnerable and I continue to feel blessed.

It's a bit of a shock when you have to admit to recognising that the people around you are ageing too.

It's almost as if your own decay might be more bearable if everyone else could retain their youth. It hits you quite hard when you come across someone you haven't seen for decades. It reminds you of your own mortality. And so it was with Tom, although, to be fair, he was looking good for his years. His white hair had disconcerted me but his skin quality was good and his eyes were as bright as ever. Fleur and Tom's wife, Ruth, got on famously from the moment they met, and once a fortnight they go shopping in Manchester, leaving Tom and me to sink a few pints.

After I retired we moved to Blackburn, partly to be near my mother but mostly because Fleur loves the place. Mum was in fine fettle with her coffee mornings and whist drives and once in a while she would join Fleur and Ruth on their trips to Manchester.

Blackburn has changed yet again. Barbara Castle Way, a great scar of urban carriageway, has sliced through the centre of town, sweeping away familiar streets. A hotel has been built in front of the railway station. God knows, the town has long needed a hotel, but this ugly carbuncle is now what you see when you come out of the station, instead of the Boulevard and the cathedral. The 'new' market has gone, to be replaced by a 'new' bus station, which is functional and dull. The precinct is still there but the market is now housed where Woolworths used to be. Fleur can buy black puddings, polony, spud pies and apple turnovers there, but I think it's soulless. Fleur says I am a reactionary. I think she may be right.

A very marked change is the declining number of pubs. A little bit of me dies when I hear about another closure. Once upon a time it seemed as if there were a pub on every corner but nowadays you pass so many that are boarded up. Once upon a time, you could navigate around the town using its pubs as landmarks. Now, there are whole areas with no pubs at all. My lament is not just about losing places for the consumption of booze. These establishments were part of a nexus of social hubs. Ben and I would be hard put to it now to find routes for our epic pub crawls.

Tom and I are in the Adelphi, near the railway station. It has been touch and go for the Adelphi over the last few years. It has closed and re-opened a few times, but it is open now and I have a special affection for the place. It was often the starting point for our Friday adventures. This morning it was an obvious place to come after seeing our wives off at the station. Tom and Ruth live out at Mellor and came in by taxi. We have a house on Buncer Lane and caught a bus. We can have a few beers without worrying about driving.

We talk about what's in the news: Brexit, Theresa May's resignation, rioting in Hong Kong and the tragic fire at Notre Dame in Paris.

This gets us on to Ben and I tell Tom about the prison visit. I tell him about Ben's last words to me: 'You're boring, Stuart, you always were.'

'Ouf,' Tom says, 'that was cruel.'

'I don't know what I'd ever said or done to provoke it,' I said.

'And you've let it rankle for - what? - thirty years?'

'More like forty,' I say. 'Oh, it's not at the front of my consciousness all the time, or even often, but it surfaces once in a while and it hurts - every time.'

'He probably didn't mean it,' Tom says.

'Oh, he meant it all right.'

'What I mean is, he probably said it because prison was getting to him,' Tom says. 'There'd be a mixture of frustration, shame and anger. He took it out on you because you were there. You shouldn't let it get to you.'

'Easily said. But thanks. It helps to get it off my chest after all these years. I couldn't tell Fleur. She has a really dim view of Ben as it is.'

'There might be an element of jealousy there, you know,' Tom says.

'Don't be daft,' I say, surprised and repelled by the idea.

'Tom,' I say, 'do you think Ben is a psychopath?'

'Why are you asking me?'

'I just thought - with your forensic experience...'

'But I'm not a criminal psychologist.'

'I know, but you must have had lots of experience of the criminal mind.'

'Well, to a point,' Tom replies. 'I don't think I'd call his behaviour psychopathic. Sociopathic maybe. There is a standard screening test but I didn't know Ben anything like as well as you did.'

'Well, you tell me about this test and I'll tell you if it applies.'

'It's a very rough tool.'

'Get on with it.'

'OK. Would you say he has a grandiose sense of self-worth?'

'No. If anything he has low self-esteem. But he was often quite cheerful about it.'

'Would you say he had an excessive need for stimulation and that he was prone to boredom?'

'Definitely. He said as much when I visited him.'

'Is he an obsessive liar?'

'Not to me. He was usually a bit too honest. He'd tell you what he thought without considering the effect.'

'Manipulative?'

'Yes, though again, not with me. He could wrap other people round his little finger. Especially girls. You've seen him operate. He had them eating out of his hands.'

'OK, a strong sign of sociopathy is a lack of empathy, what they call "shallow affect".'

'What does that mean?'

'It means a lack of emotion when an emotional response is appropriate. You could call it callousness.'

'Yes, I think that applies.'

'What about poor behavioural control? Impulsiveness?'

'No,' I say. 'On the contrary. I would say that Ben was a meticulous planner. At least where his incendiary activities were concerned.'

'Parasitic lifestyle?'

'Yes.'

'Cruelty to animals?'

'Not so far as I know.'

'Promiscuous sexual behaviour?'

'I think we both know the answer to that one.'

'High levels of irresponsibility?'

'Without wanting to sound like a prig, definitely.'

'Here's a good one: "Revocation of Conditional Release"?

'Which means?'

'It means a tendency to screw up even when given a break.'

'Categorically yes.'

'That's all I can remember,' Tom says.

'So what's the conclusion?' I ask.

'I don't know. What do you think?'

'A mix of yes and no?'

'Exactly. Any marked preponderance?'

'No. Roughly equal.'

'Well, there you are. I told you it was a rough tool. And another thing. If you try the test yourself you'll conclude that you're a howling psycho yourself and should be put away. Your round, I think.'

I am disappointed, I have to say. I hoped somehow to pin Ben down, to find a way to explain how and why his life had gone all wrong.

I return with the beers and we talk of other things: our shape-shifting town, the decline of the North, the way words transmute so that they come to mean the opposite of what they used to mean. Words like 'liberal' and 'élite'.

At length Tom says: 'I'd better make a move. I promised her Ladyship I'd have tea ready when she gets home. I just hope she hasn't spent all our money on shoes. What is it with women and shoes?'

'God knows,' I say, as we emerge from the pub. 'Oh shit, it's raining.'

'Right, I'd better run for it - or what passes for running these days. Oh, and Stuart...'

'What?'

'Don't beat yourself up,' Tom says. 'You're not boring.'

33.   EPILOGUE

THE FIRE IN NOTRE DAME hit me hard. I was so vexed with the kind of moron who said 'it's only a church', and even more angry with the 'educated' morons who said: 'the *flèche* is nineteenth-century: it's not even medieval'. Well, so bloody what? The cathedral is a cultural icon all over the world, a repository of history, a symbol at the heart of Paris, at the heart of France. Think what it has seen down the centuries. Fleur shed streams of tears and was inconsolable.

A few months later, a fire at St John's Church in Blackburn hit me even harder. Obviously, it did not have the history of Notre Dame, but it had stood at the bottom of Richmond Terrace for three hundred years and was the oldest church in Blackburn. I felt it personally: a part of my childhood had gone up in flames; it was like a diminution of my identity. Even though it had been deconsecrated in the seventies and had served more recently as an arts centre, the fire nonetheless left a hole in my past. When both of your parents are dead, you realise there are multitudes of questions you didn't ask them that you can never, ever ask them now. The past is always there, but it is not always accessible, and when you can no longer reach it, there is only the fleeting present and the shrinking future.

Fleur and I had been in France at the time, and I didn't hear about it till we reached home. I have seen the photographs and they are terrible. My heart lurched to see the roof gone, flames belching out of the high half-moon windows, and a pall of black smoke hanging over the nave, the tower and its cupola a grey silhouette against a hideous orange glow. Beyond is the serene cobalt sky of an April dusk.

A photograph of the interior is even more heart-breaking. The flat Ionic pillars on either side of the chancel and the arch above, once dazzling white, are scorched and blackened. The window depicting the crucifixion, above what was the altar, has somehow survived, but the sanctuary is trashed and a charred beam has fallen across it. The choir stalls, where Ben used to pull faces at me during Evensong, are gone.

Nobody knows if the church can be restored. The official line is that the fire started from an electrical fault, but I can't help wondering. I have not seen Ben since that prison visit nearly forty years ago. Nobody seems to know where he is, or if he ever returned to Blackburn.

I can't help wondering because I can't forget when we played hide and seek in the graveyard outside. I can't forget the incident of the firework which landed Ben in Casualty. I can't forget racing round the galleries, the wooden galleries that must have been so combustible. Most of all, I can't forget the time we got inside the organ and Ben said - what had he said? - 'If I lit a fire in here, it would go up like I don't know what! I can see it now, blazing - with the organ playing.'

I wish someone could tell me how, when we were inseparable in our early years, when people took us for twins, when, at times, we could hardly breathe for laughing, how our lives could fork so dramatically, how I managed to arrive at a modest kind of success - despite being a little boring - while Ben became so utterly fallen. I can't help wondering whether he thought his brief ecstasies in the face of the conflagrations he had himself created were somehow compensation for the wasted years.

Fleur and I went to check out the remains of the church. There wasn't much to see. There were railings around the site. The absence of the roof was shocking, as were the blind windows. I could say nothing to Fleur but in my heart there was a sharp sense of loss, and not just for the church.

In spite of everything, down the ephemeral rush of the years, I miss my friend.

ACKNOWLEDGMENTS

As I was bringing my work on this novel to a close, I learnt that the insurers were going to pay out for the restoration of St John's Church, Blackburn, following the fire in 2019. I was pleased about this, partly because I didn't think they would, and partly because it is an iconic building in the centre of a town which has already lost too much of its history at the hands of philistine developers.

Like Stuart and Ben, I was a choirboy there many years ago, and I have many happy memories of that time. Of course, I am real while Stuart and Ben are not, except in my imagination and now yours.

Once again I am grateful to Peter Cheshire for his scrupulous editing which has been backed up by careful research. His sympathetic reading has been a great encouragement. My thanks go to Julie Dexter again too. Her advice from across the pond is particularly valuable. Among many other things she has helped me iron out syntax on which a reader might have stumbled. Michael Rogers proof-read the text with professional exactitude and he has my warmest appreciation. I am thrice-blest to have such generous and accomplished help in bringing my story into the light of day.

I am indebted also to two closed Facebook groups: *Blackburn and District in the Past* and *1960's Blackburn - Where are you now?* Photographs and memories posted by members have been a great inspiration. Thanks to administrators Frank Riding and Barbara Whewell Lawrence respectively for their permission to promote my books on the sites and for their encouragement.

Finally, a big thank you to Steve Brown, archivist at the Blackburn Fire Brigade for helping me track down the copyright for the cover photograph to *The Lancashire Telegraph*, and to the Editor, Steve Thompson, for permission to use it.

I have tried to be accurate in my depiction of the town. If there are any inaccuracies, they will be down to flawed memory rather than wilful misrepresentation.

London
September 2021

Printed in Poland
by Amazon Fulfillment
Poland Sp. z o.o., Wrocław
17 October 2021

3f820f31-04e5-4033-8819-3bde9b5d851cR01